A HORSE SHE DOESN'T LIKE?

"Hey there, Ditto," Carole said to attract the horse's attention. To her surprise, he started. Then, with a snort, he whirled around to face her. "Whoa! Sorry, didn't mean to scare you." Carole tried to make her voice as quiet and unthreatening as possible. "Come here, boy." She held out her hand for the horse to sniff.

Ditto regarded her suspiciously for a long moment. Finally he stretched his neck forward, not moving his feet an inch, and quickly snuffled Carole's hand. Just as quickly, he jerked his head back again.

Carole withdrew her hand. "Wow, you seem a little jittery for a camp horse," she said. "I guess it must be all the excitement of the first day. But don't worry, I'm sure we're going to be great friends before long. I never met a horse I didn't like."

THE SADDLE CLUB

SUMMER HORSE

BONNIE BRYANT

A SKYLARK BOOK

NEW YORK • TORONTO • LONDON • SYDNEY • AUCKLAND

RL 5, 009–012

SUMMER HORSE

A Bantam Skylark Book/July 1997

ISBN 0-553-48422-2

Published simultaneously in the United States and Canada.

*I would like to express my special thanks
to Catherine Hapka for her help
in the writing of this book.*

"COME ON, CAROLE," Stevie Lake said. "Stop whispering sweet nothings into Starlight's ear and get him ready to go. I'm in the mood for a trail ride."

Carole Hanson looked over the top of the stall door at Stevie, who was grinning at her from outside. "Very funny," Carole said, continuing to stroke her horse's soft nose. "You know very well we can't go until Lisa gets here."

Lisa Atwood was their friend and the third founding member of The Saddle Club. The three girls had formed the club after they had met and become friends at Pine Hollow Stables. The Saddle Club had only two rules:

1

Members had to be horse-crazy, and they had to be willing to help one another with any problem, great or small.

Stevie leaned against the stall door, stretching to give Starlight, a handsome bay gelding, a pat on the neck. "I'm just kidding," she said. "I know exactly how you feel. I missed Belle while we were away, too." The Saddle Club had returned a few days earlier from a visit to the Bar None, a dude ranch out West that was owned by the parents of a friend of theirs. Belle was Stevie's horse, a lively bay mare.

Just then a familiar voice came from behind Stevie. "Ahem."

The girls turned and saw Max Regnery, the owner and manager of Pine Hollow, standing in the aisle with his hands on his hips.

"Oh, hi, Max," Stevie said, sounding a little guilty. She knew Max hated seeing riders standing around talking when there were stable chores to be done. And there were *always* stable chores to be done. Riders were expected to help with everything that went into running the stable, from mucking out stalls to cleaning tack to sweeping the aisles. That way Max didn't have to hire a lot of extra stable hands and could keep fees down.

"Hi, Stevie," Max said. He glanced into Starlight's

stall. "Hello, Carole. What are you girls up to? You look a little bored."

"Oh, no, Max," Stevie replied quickly. "We're just waiting for Lisa. She should be here any minute—any second, really. You know how she is. She's never late."

"Well, how about if you wait for her in the tack room?" Max suggested. "There's a box of irons in there that could use cleaning and sorting."

The girls knew better than to argue. Carole said goodbye to Starlight, and soon she and Stevie were seated on a couple of trunks in the tack room with a cardboard box on the floor between them.

"Don't worry," Stevie said as she searched through the box for a match to the stirrup iron she was holding. "Soon we'll be at camp, and you know what that means—a whole month of rest from all these chores, courtesy of the Moose Hill stable hands." All three members of The Saddle Club were leaving for Moose Hill Riding Camp the following week. They had been to Moose Hill before, and they agreed that it was one of their favorite places in the entire world. This year for the first time, the camp was offering monthlong sessions in addition to the usual two weeks, and The Saddle Club had signed up for one of the longer sessions immediately.

Carole really didn't mind pitching in around the stable, but she had to admit it would be nice to take a break for a while. "I think we should still take care of our own horses, though," she said.

"Sure," Stevie said with a shrug. "That goes without saying. But at least we won't have to do boring stuff like sorting irons." She tossed the irons she had just polished and tied together into one of the trunks. "It will practically be a life of leisure. That's what our parents are paying the big bucks for, right?"

Carole nodded, looking worried. "I guess so."

Stevie noticed her friend's expression. "What's the matter?"

Carole shrugged and leaned over to get another pair of irons out of the box. "Nothing, really," she said. "It's just that I didn't realize camp was going to be so expensive this year. And since I'm taking Starlight, it adds up even more." Moose Hill campers had a choice of bringing their own horses or riding the ones owned by the camp. This year Stevie and Carole were planning to bring their own horses. Lisa, who didn't have a horse of her own and normally rode a Pine Hollow horse named Prancer, was going to ride a camp horse.

"I guess the prices did go up," Stevie said. "Now that I think about it, my parents complained about it when they got the bill the other day."

"My dad didn't complain, exactly," Carole said. "But I saw his face when he opened the bill. He didn't look very happy." Carole's father was a colonel in the Marine Corps. He made a comfortable living, but he wasn't as well-to-do as Stevie's parents, who were both lawyers. Carole knew that her father always tried to give her everything she needed. But she also knew that most of what she wanted had to do with horses, and horses were expensive.

"My mom and dad never look happy when they open bills," Stevie said. "Don't worry about it."

Carole wiped dirt off the iron she was holding. "I can't help worrying," she said. "What if camp costs too much this year? Maybe Dad's just trying to figure out how to break it to me that I can't go."

"This is your father we're talking about, remember?" Stevie said, giving her friend a look of genuine surprise. "Since when does he keep something like that to himself?"

"You're right," Carole said. "He would have told me." Ever since her mother had died a few years earlier, Carole and her father had been closer than before. She knew he wouldn't keep really bad news from her, such as not being able to send her to camp. "But what if it costs just enough to make him worry?"

"I don't know," Stevie said. She dropped another set of irons into the trunk. "Maybe you should talk to him about it."

"I think I will," Carole said. "If I don't, I'll probably worry the whole time I'm at camp, and I won't be able to enjoy myself."

Stevie leaned back and smiled. "Now, that's one thing I'm not worried about," she said dreamily. "I know I'm going to enjoy every minute of camp."

"That wouldn't have anything to do with a certain young fellow named Phil, would it?" Carole asked. Despite her own worries, she couldn't resist teasing Stevie about her boyfriend, Phil Marsten. The couple had met during The Saddle Club's first stay at Moose Hill.

Stevie grinned. "Maybe," she admitted. "But don't tell Belle—you know how jealous she can be." She sighed happily. "It's going to be so great. We'll have a whole month to go for romantic trail rides through the woods, help each other with our dressage training, spend hours together grooming our horses . . ."

"If you and Phil are going to be doing all that together, I think Belle might begin to suspect something," Carole pointed out.

Stevie hardly heard her. She was too busy thinking over all the plans she had made. "We'll even be able to reenact our very first date. We walked down to the pond that first night at camp, remember?" She sighed again. "It's going to be great to spend so much time with him."

Carole nodded understandingly. Phil lived about ten miles away from the girls' hometown of Willow Creek, so he and Stevie were only able to see each other occasionally.

A few minutes later Carole stood up and stretched. The box of irons was almost empty. "We're just about done here," she said. She glanced at her watch. "I wonder what's keeping Lisa? It's not like her to be late. You did tell her to meet us at ten o'clock, right?"

Before Stevie could answer, Max came into the tack room. He peered into the box and nodded, looking satisfied. "Nice work, girls," he said. "I don't know what I'm going to do without you for a whole month. Who am I going to turn to when it's time to hose down the manure pit?"

Stevie shuddered, but Carole just frowned. Max's comment had reminded her about the cost of camp. "I almost wish we had to do that at Moose Hill, too," she muttered.

Max looked surprised. "Am I hearing things?" he said. "Don't tell me you're not looking forward to being waited on hand and hoof by the Moose Hill staff." He spoke lightly, but Carole and Stevie knew that he disapproved of that aspect of the way Moose Hill was run.

Max believed that riding meant more than climbing in and out of a saddle, and that a good rider was involved in every aspect of horse care, even the tedious and unpleasant ones.

"I wouldn't mind getting waited on a little less if it meant camp cost a little less," Carole admitted. She told Max about her worries.

Max nodded. "Believe me, I understand your concern," he said. "Moose Hill's prices *have* gone up quite a bit since last year, especially the boarding fees. I was thinking about sending Prancer to camp with Lisa— Prancer could use the intensive kind of work she'd get there. But when I found out how much it would cost, I changed my mind." He shook his head. "I don't know exactly what's going on at Moose Hill, but they seem to be making a lot of changes."

"Changes?" Stevie said, finishing the irons and dropping them into the trunk. "What kind of changes?"

"Well, there's the new monthlong session, for one," Max said. "Also, I understand they've added more cabins to allow them to take in more campers. And there are new tennis courts and so forth." He paused, noticing Carole's and Stevie's surprised expressions. "Didn't you read the brochure?"

The two girls exchanged looks. "Uh, not really," Carole admitted. "I think Lisa might have. But I was too excited to bother."

"Me too," Stevie said. "Besides, we've been there before. I didn't think the brochure would tell me anything I didn't know."

Carole was back to thinking about her own problem. "I just can't believe this is happening," she said. "I don't want to feel guilty every time I look at Starlight while I'm there. I'm really looking forward to riding him nonstop for a month, especially after a whole week without him at the Bar None. I really missed him."

Max looked thoughtful. "Carole, I have a suggestion for you."

"What is it?" Carole asked eagerly. She knew Max's suggestions were almost always good ones.

"Well, I'm not sure you're going to like it," Max said, sitting down on a trunk near the girls. "You know I always say a good rider can ride any horse well, right?"

Carole and Stevie nodded. It was one of Max's favorite sayings.

Just then they all heard footsteps approaching. A moment later, Lisa walked into the tack room. "Hello, Lisa," Max greeted her. "I'm glad you're here. You're the perfect example of what I was just about to say." He turned back to Carole. "Lisa rides Prancer most of the time, but occasionally she has to take a turn on a different horse. Those occasions help her ride Prancer better. Not having her own horse has almost certainly helped Lisa progress so fast as a rider." Lisa hadn't been riding as long as either of her friends, but she had learned quickly. "Learning to ride all sorts of horses is good for her progress—for anybody's progress. No matter how long she's been riding."

"I think I know what you're saying," Carole said. "And you were right. I don't like it. What's the point of going to camp just to be miserable? I can't imagine being there without Starlight."

Stevie nodded sympathetically. She hadn't owned Belle as long as Carole had owned Starlight, but she knew exactly how her friend felt. It would be terrible to go to camp and leave her horse behind.

Max just shrugged. "I'm not telling you what to do, Carole," he said quietly. "I'm just saying that it wouldn't hurt for you to have some of that kind of learning once in a while."

"I just did, remember?" Carole pointed out. "I spent a whole week riding a different horse at the Bar None."

"You know that's not the same thing," Max said. "That was just a few days of riding for fun. This will be four weeks of intensive training and learning." He held up a hand. "I can see a month without Starlight is out of the question. But I have another idea."

Carole glanced at her two friends, then back at Max. "What is it?" she asked apprehensively.

"It's sort of a compromise," Max said. "If you want to ride a camp horse for the first two weeks of camp, I'll arrange to have Starlight brought down to Moose Hill for the second two weeks. That way you'll get a good amount of experience on another horse, but you'll be able to enjoy your own horse, too."

Carole bit her lip. "Leave Starlight here for two weeks? That would mean I'd save . . . hmmm . . ." She quickly figured out the savings in her head. It was a substantial amount, even after figuring in Starlight's usual Pine Hollow boarding fees. "Wow," she said. "Maybe it would be worth it." She took a deep breath. "I'll do it, Max. And not just because of the money. You're right—it will be good for me."

"Carole, are you sure about this?" Stevie cried.

"I'm sure," Carole said. She managed a weak grin. "I'll be fine on one of the camp horses. After all, I never met a horse I didn't like."

"I think you'll be glad you did this, Carole," Max said. "And don't worry about arranging the change in plans with Moose Hill. I'll call them right now and get it all settled."

11

"Thanks, Max," Carole said. She was already wondering if she'd made the right decision. But when she pictured her father's worried face as he opened the camp bill, her doubts faded. Max hurried out of the tack room, and Carole decided it was time to take her mind off the whole situation. Luckily she knew the perfect way to do that. "Now that you're here, Lisa, let's tack up and go," she said. "We've got some serious trail riding to do."

Carole glanced at her friend and stopped. For the first time she realized that Lisa hadn't said a word since coming into the room. Now she saw that Lisa looked upset enough to cry.

Stevie had just noticed Lisa's expression, too. "What is it?" she asked, hurrying over to her friend. "What's wrong, Lisa?"

Lisa gulped. "I—I got some bad news," she began.

Stevie and Carole exchanged worried glances. "What is it?" Carole asked gently.

Lisa sniffled. "My report card came in the mail."

"Yeah, mine too," Carole said. She and Lisa attended the public school in town. Stevie went to private school and had received her report card on her last day of school. "And?"

"And—" Lisa sniffled again. "And I got a B-plus in math."

12

"And?" Stevie prompted, still waiting for the bad news.

Lisa looked surprised. "Didn't you hear me? I got a B-plus. I was expecting an A."

"That's your terrible news?" Carole asked. She let out a sigh of relief, then chuckled. "I was afraid someone died or something."

Lisa frowned. "This is no laughing matter."

Stevie knew that Lisa took her schoolwork and her straight-A average seriously, but she still couldn't believe she was so upset. "Come on," she said, putting an arm around Lisa. "Don't take it so hard. It's summer, remember? Time to forget about school and have fun. Who cares about grades when it's a beautiful day and the trails beckon?"

Lisa shrugged away Stevie's arm. "*I* care. This was an accelerated math class. That means it will go on my permanent school transcript. When I apply to college in a few years, that B-plus is going to be there for everyone to see." She ran a hand through her light brown hair. "Besides, if I can't handle the work I'm doing now, how am I going to manage the kinds of advanced courses I'll be taking in the next few years?"

"Nobody says you have to take advanced courses," Stevie said.

"Yes, I do," Lisa replied. "If I want to do well on the SATs, I have to learn the material."

Carole's eyes widened. The SATs? Those were the standardized tests people took before applying to college. They were years and years away. Why was Lisa getting so worked up about them now? Suddenly she thought of one possible reason. "Lisa," she said hesitantly, "was your mother upset about your grade, too?"

Stevie glanced quickly at Carole, then waited for Lisa's response. Mrs. Atwood sometimes put a lot of pressure on her daughter. She had made Lisa take classes and lessons in everything from painting to ballet, and she could be unreasonable when Lisa said no. Lately things had seemed a lot better between Lisa and her mother, but maybe this was a sign that they were taking a turn for the worse.

But Lisa shook her head. "Mom didn't think a B-plus was so bad. She just doesn't understand."

Carole and Stevie again exchanged confused glances. Lisa was obviously upset, and they wanted to help her. But they didn't really understand, either.

"Let's go for that trail ride," Carole suggested tentatively. "Maybe it will make you feel better."

Lisa shrugged. "All right, let's go," she said glumly. "But I don't think anything will make me feel better right now. My perfect A average is ruined forever."

14

The following Sunday morning, Lisa tucked her riding boots on top of the clothes in her suitcase and zipped it up. She carried the suitcase downstairs to the front hall and set it by the door. Two other bags were already there.

"What time is Red picking you up, dear?" Mrs. Atwood asked, hurrying toward her from the kitchen.

Lisa glanced at her watch. "He should be here any minute." Red O'Malley, Pine Hollow's head stable hand, was driving The Saddle Club and Belle to camp.

Mrs. Atwood held up a bulging package wrapped in aluminum foil. "Here are some homemade cookies," she said. "I thought you and your friends would like to have them for all your late-night chats."

Lisa rolled her eyes. "They do feed us at camp, Mom," she said. Mrs. Atwood had already tucked several bags of candy and other treats into Lisa's bags.

Mrs. Atwood didn't pay any attention. She hurried over and unzipped Lisa's blue duffel bag. "I'll just put them in— Oh, my!" she said, taking a closer look at the contents of the bag. "How many books are you taking to camp, Lisa?"

"I told you," Lisa said. "They're the books on my summer reading list." Lisa was taking an accelerated English class in the fall, and the teacher had sent the students a list of suggested titles for summer reading. There were twenty books on the list, and Lisa had packed all twenty in the duffel bag.

"I didn't realize you were bringing *all* the books with you," Mrs. Atwood said. "You'll never have time to read them all."

"I'm going to be there for a whole month." Lisa took the bag from her mother and zipped it closed again. "And there's always lots of free time at camp. I'll have plenty of time to read."

Mrs. Atwood looked uncertain. "Well, if you say so . . ."

Lisa unzipped the bag again and rummaged around

inside. "Actually, I should probably get a book out now," she said, talking more to herself than to her mother. "Red will probably put my bags in the back, and I want to get started on my reading on the way to camp."

At that, Mrs. Atwood burst out laughing. "Oh, come now, dear," she exclaimed. "You must be joking. You know as well as I do that from the minute you set foot in that van until the time you get to camp, you and your friends are going to be gabbing a mile a minute about your horses and your riding and so forth."

Lisa frowned. It was true that The Saddle Club generally did a lot of talking when they got together. But the least her mother could do was be a little more supportive of her desire to try to get some work done. She made it sound as though she thought Lisa had no willpower at all, as if she almost *wanted* her to fail. "Not this time," Lisa replied firmly. She pulled her copy of *The Scarlet Letter* out of the bag and tucked it under her arm. "I want to get a head start on this class so I won't end up with a bad grade like I did in math class."

"Oh, Lisa," Mrs. Atwood said with a sigh. "Are you still thinking about that B-plus? I really don't think you—"

But the rest of her words were cut off by a honk from outside. Red had arrived. Lisa gathered up her bags and hurried out, barely pausing to kiss her mother good-bye.

* * *

AN HOUR LATER, Stevie pointed out the window of the van. "There it is!" she shrieked. "Right ahead of us—the road to Moose Hill. Don't miss it, Red!"

Red rolled his eyes as he turned the van onto the side road. "Don't worry, Stevie," he said. "I wouldn't dare miss the turn. If I did, it would mean that much more time trapped in this van with you three chatterboxes."

Stevie stuck out her tongue at him, and all three girls laughed. They *had* been talking almost nonstop since leaving Willow Creek, but they knew Red didn't really mind, especially since they were talking about horses.

"I miss him already," Carole said, returning to their previous topic, namely, her decision to leave Starlight at home for the first two weeks of camp. "But I know I'll learn a lot, like Max said."

"Besides, think about how much your dad appreciates it," Lisa reminded her.

Carole smiled. "I know," she said. "That's the best part. He never actually came out and said he was worried before, but that didn't stop him from thanking me for being so thoughtful and responsible."

"You'll probably end up riding Basil again," Stevie said. "You really liked him, right?"

"Definitely," Carole said. Basil was the friendly, well-trained horse Carole had ridden at Moose Hill before she owned Starlight. She decided she wouldn't mind getting reacquainted with him at all. "He's the next best thing to Starlight. I hope Barry remembers how much I liked him."

"He will," Stevie said confidently. Barry was the manager of Moose Hill. He was a friendly, caring man who did his best to make his campers happy. And he knew almost as much about horses as Max did. "No matter how much bigger Moose Hill is, you can count on Barry to keep track of everything and everyone, just like always."

Carole frowned at the reminder that things at the camp had changed since last summer. "I wonder what else is different besides more cabins," she said.

"According to the brochure, they've added a lot more recreational facilities," Lisa said.

Stevie and Carole grinned. Count on Lisa to have actually read the camp's brochure—and to use a phrase like *recreational facilities*. "Like what?" Stevie asked.

"Tennis courts, volleyball nets—things like that," Lisa said. "Just about the only thing they don't have now is an indoor pool."

Carole shuddered. "I certainly hope not!" she exclaimed. "It wouldn't feel like Moose Hill if we went swimming anywhere but in the pond." The cabins at the camp were clustered around a swimming pond with a small, sandy beach. It was the perfect place to cool off after a long, hot day of riding.

Lisa glanced out the window. The paved part of the road had ended, and Red was guiding the van slowly over the hard-packed dirt trail that wound its way through a forest of stately maples.

"The camp may have improved since last year," he said, clenching his teeth as the vehicle dipped into an especially large rut, "but the road sure hasn't. If anything, it's gotten even worse."

Stevie glanced at the road ahead. She noticed a long, shiny black sedan pulled off to one side. It was so far off the road that it was almost hidden in the trees. "I guess you're not the only one who doesn't like the road, Red," she said, pointing.

Carole glanced at the car and giggled. "That's not exactly the car I'd bring to drop my kids off at riding camp," she said. "It looks like something out of one of those old gangster films my dad likes."

"Who says gangsters' kids can't be riders, too?" Stevie said.

Lisa was looking ahead. "Look, there's the gate," she said. "We're almost there." Red drove through the open horse gate and up a hill. When they reached the crest, Moose Hill Riding Camp lay spread out below them.

"We're here! We're here!" Stevie exclaimed, bouncing

20

up and down on the seat. "Moose Hill, here we come!" When they reached the trail leading down to the cabins, Red brought the van to a halt.

"First stop," he said. "Out you get."

Lisa and Carole hopped out and headed for the back of the van to get their things. They had promised to carry Stevie's suitcase to the cabin while she and Red settled Belle in at the stable. As she pulled her duffel bag out, Lisa tucked *The Scarlet Letter* into it. She hadn't had a chance to read a single page—just as her mother had predicted, she realized with a flash of annoyance. She would have to do better if she expected to get through the whole reading list by the end of camp.

Carole was out of breath by the time she and Lisa reached Cabin Three. She was lugging Stevie's suitcase as well as her own, since Lisa had three bags to carry. "Thank goodness we're here," she gasped. "I'm ready for lights-out already." She rubbed her hands on her jeans, then looked up and noticed that Lisa was staring at a sheaf of papers pinned to the cabin door. "What's that?" she asked.

"It's a list of campers," Lisa said slowly. "It tells which cabin everybody is in. Your name is listed under Cabin Three, and so is Stevie's. But I'm listed under Cabin Six!"

"THERE HAS TO BE some kind of mistake," Carole said. "Let me see." But when she looked at the list, she saw that Lisa was right.

Lisa's lower lip quivered a little. "I thought we requested the same cabin," she said.

"We did," Carole said firmly. "And what's more, Barry knows us. He would never separate us. I'm sure it's just a typo or something." She opened the door of the cabin and set down her suitcase and Stevie's. Nobody else was there at the moment. "Come on, put your stuff down and let's go see Barry."

Lisa obeyed. The two girls hurried up the sloping trail to the rec hall, where Barry's office was located. Luckily, he was there.

"Carole Hanson and Lisa Atwood!" he exclaimed when he saw them. "I thought you'd never arrive."

But Carole didn't stop to return the greeting. "Barry, we have a problem," she said. "Lisa's been assigned to the wrong cabin." Quickly, she explained the situation.

Barry rubbed his chin. "This shouldn't have happened," he muttered. "I knew I should have checked those lists more carefully." He sighed. "I'm very sorry, girls. My old assistant left over the winter, and the new one is still getting adjusted. He must have made a mistake in the cabin assignments."

"But you can fix it, right?" Lisa asked.

Barry dug through a pile of papers on his desk until he found a copy of the list. He read it over, then sighed again. "I'm afraid not," he said. "The camp is completely full this session, and a lot of the other girls asked to bunk together, too. It wouldn't be fair to start moving people around now."

Carole couldn't believe her ears. "It isn't fair that Lisa has to be in a different cabin, either," she cried. "There must be something we can do. Maybe we can talk to some of the others, see what we can work out—"

"I don't think so," Barry said abruptly, cutting her off. He glanced toward the hallway, where a man in a dark suit was waiting. "I'm sorry, girls, but I've got a meeting right now. The best I can do is promise to fix this after the first two weeks. Some of the kids are leaving then, and that should free up enough space to work something out."

"Two weeks?" Lisa repeated in disbelief. Was she really going to have to spend two whole weeks in a strange cabin, away from her best friends?

"Two weeks," Barry repeated. "Sorry, but that's my best offer." He stood up, and there was nothing the girls could do but leave the office.

Stevie was waiting for them at Cabin Three. "Wow, you should see all the horses at the stable!" she exclaimed as soon as she saw them. "I guess I didn't realize that a lot more campers meant a lot more horses, too. But Belle is all settled in her stall, and. . . ." Her voice trailed off as she noticed the looks on her friends' faces. "What's wrong?"

Carole told her about the cabin mix-up and Barry's response to it. "It wasn't like him at all," she finished. "He practically threw us out of his office after hardly trying to help."

"This is awful," Stevie declared. She put her arm

around Lisa, who was trying not to cry. "Don't worry, Lisa. You can stay here with Carole. I'll go to Cabin Six instead."

"Or we could take turns," Carole suggested. "Switch off between this cabin and that one."

Lisa shook her head, trying her best to get herself under control. The situation was bad, but it was nothing to cry about. "Don't be silly," she said, glad that her voice sounded almost normal. "I appreciate the offers, but I'll be okay. It's only for two weeks, right?"

"Well, if you're sure," Stevie said reluctantly. "But I'm going to talk to Barry about this myself the next time I see him."

Lisa smiled, feeling a little better. Stevie was an expert at convincing adults to do things they didn't want to do. If anyone could solve this problem, Stevie could. "Thanks. In the meantime, how about helping me move my stuff to Cabin Six?"

Stevie grunted as she lifted Lisa's duffel bag. "What do you have in here?" she asked. "Bricks?"

"Books," Lisa replied. She explained about her summer reading list.

"Oh, is that why you had that book with you in the van?" Carole said. "I just assumed it was something your mother made you bring."

"I can't believe you want to spend that much time reading when there are so many better things to do," Stevie said.

Lisa shrugged. "It doesn't matter if I want to or not," she said. "I have to—if I want to do well in the class next year, that is. And I do."

"Whatever," Stevie said. "But you won't catch *me* doing homework at camp. I guarantee it."

Carole laughed. "It's hard to catch you doing it at home, either."

"Well, I wouldn't want to upset my parents by getting any B-pluses," Stevie replied with a grin, giving Lisa a sly glance. "They're totally accustomed to Cs!" She craned her neck, looking around as the three girls approached Cabin Six.

Carole reached out and grabbed Stevie's arm just in time to keep her from tripping over a stone in the path. "Watch it," she said. "What are you looking for?"

"Phil," Stevie said. "I was kind of expecting him to be at the stable to meet me. Teddy's there already, but there's no sign of his owner." Teddy was Phil's horse.

"I'm sure you'll see him soon." Carole stopped in front of Cabin Six. "Well, here we are," she said, trying to sound cheerful.

Lisa reached for the door, but it swung open before she could touch it. A very tall, slender girl started to step out, stopping short just in time to avoid running into Lisa. She looked about a year or two older than Lisa, and she was one of the prettiest girls The Saddle Club had ever seen.

"Oops," she said. "Sorry. I didn't know anyone was coming in."

"That's okay," Lisa said. "My name's Lisa Atwood. Um, I guess we're going to be cabin mates." She stuck out her hand.

The other girl shook it. "I'm Piper Sullivan," she replied with a smile. "It's nice to meet you. I'll catch you later, okay? I was just on my way to the stable to check on my horse."

"Bye," Lisa said. Then she led the way inside.

"She seemed nice," Carole said, as Lisa set her bags on one of the wooden bunks. "Maybe this won't be so bad after all."

"Come on," Lisa said. "I'll unpack later. Let's go check out the stable."

When the girls entered the stable, they found another list hanging near the door. This one noted which campers would be riding which horses. Lisa found her name quickly. To her delight, the name next to hers was a familiar one.

"I got Major again," she said. She had ridden the steady bay gelding on her first trip to Moose Hill.

27

"Do you see my name?" Carole asked. "Did I get Basil?" She searched the list until she found her name. Originally the word *outside* had been typed next to it, and she guessed that that was left over from when they had thought she was bringing Starlight. But that had been crossed out, and the name *Ditto* was written in pencil beside it.

"Ditto," she said blankly. "I don't remember any horse here called Ditto."

"Must be new," Stevie said. She was still keeping a watch for Phil.

Carole shrugged. "I wonder why I didn't get Basil?" She scanned the list. "I don't see his name with any of the other campers. If he's still unassigned, maybe I can request him." She looked around for someone to ask, but all she saw were a few other campers. "Where are all the stable hands?"

Lisa looked, too. "I don't see any," she said. "That's strange. Usually the place is crawling with them."

Stevie wandered over and glanced down the aisle where Teddy was stabled. Phil wasn't there, but someone else she knew was. "Hi, Betty," she called. Betty was one of the senior instructors at the camp. She taught all the jumping classes.

"Hi, Stevie," she said. "Good to see you. Are your friends here, too?"

28

"Come see for yourself," Stevie said.

When the instructor joined them, Carole asked her about Basil. Betty's smile faded a little. "Oh, I'm sorry, Carole," she said. "I remember how well you and Basil got along. But he's not here anymore. He was sold over the winter."

"Sold?" Carole repeated, surprised and disappointed. "But why?"

Betty looked down at the water bucket she was carrying. "Uh, I'm not really sure," she said. "But don't worry, I'm sure you and Ditto will get along just fine. He's new and seems to have a mind of his own, but we figured you're a good rider and could handle him." Betty pointed the way to Ditto's stall, then hurried away with a wave.

"Come on, let's go check him out," Lisa said. "I want to say hi to Major, too."

"I'll meet you there in a minute," Stevie promised. "I just want to look in on Belle." Carole and Lisa suspected that their friend actually wanted to take another look around for Phil, but they didn't say so. While Stevie hurried off, they found Ditto's stall. As it turned out, Major was just a few stalls down. While Lisa greeted her mount fondly, Carole decided to go ahead and get acquainted with hers.

Ditto was a nice-looking Appaloosa gelding. When Carole peeked over the half door of his stall, the horse was facing the back wall, munching peacefully on some hay.

"Hey there, Ditto," Carole said to attract his attention. To her surprise, the horse started. Then, with a snort, he whirled around to face her. "Whoa! Sorry, didn't mean to scare you." Carole tried to make her voice as quiet and unthreatening as possible. "Come here, boy." She held out her hand for the horse to sniff.

Ditto regarded her suspiciously for a long moment. Finally he stretched his neck forward, not moving his feet an inch, and quickly snuffled Carole's hand. Just as quickly, he jerked his head back again.

Carole withdrew her hand. "Wow, you seem a little jittery for a camp horse," she said. "I guess it must be all the excitement of the first day. But don't worry, I'm sure we're going to be great friends before long. I never met a horse I didn't like."

Stevie arrived just in time to hear Carole's last comment. "I'd say that's the understatement of the year," she said. She frowned. "I still can't find Phil. He's not in the stable."

"Then there's just one solution," Carole said.

Stevie looked hopeful. "What's that?"

Carole smiled. "*Leave* the stable. Come on, it's almost lunchtime anyway. And you know Phil never misses a meal—it's a foolproof plan." She linked her arm through

Stevie's and walked down the aisle to Major's stall. "Ready, Lisa?"

"Sure," Lisa said from inside the stall. "As long as the next place we go is to lunch. I'm starving." She gave Major a farewell pat and joined her friends in the aisle.

Just then The Saddle Club heard hoofbeats. They turned to see Piper Sullivan, the girl from Lisa's cabin, leading a long-legged, coal-black mare out of one of the stalls.

Piper smiled when she saw them. "Hello again," she said.

"Is that your horse?" Carole asked breathlessly. She couldn't take her eyes off of the mare, which was every bit as beautiful as her owner.

Piper nodded. "Her name's Tapestry," she said, her eyes shining as she looked at her horse.

Carole knew that look. It was the same one she had every time she looked at Starlight, and she felt a pang as she thought about him. But she forced herself to smile at Piper. "She's gorgeous," she said sincerely. "Is she a Thoroughbred?"

Piper nodded again. "We're just going for a quick ride."

"But it's almost lunchtime," Stevie said. She grinned. "And believe me, the way Moose Hill campers usually eat, you don't want to be late, or all you'll get is scraps."

"Thanks for the tip," Piper said with a chuckle. "But Tap really needs to stretch her legs. She had a long ride here this morning."

The girls nodded understandingly. There wasn't one among them who wouldn't be late for a meal—or even skip one entirely—when a horse's comfort was at stake. They watched as Piper led Tapestry past them toward the stable entrance, then followed more slowly.

The girls had to walk past Ditto's stall on their way out. Carole noticed that the Appaloosa had come to the front of the stall when Piper and her horse walked by. He was still there, looking out over the door. "Oh, so you decided to be sociable after all, hmmm?" she said. She reached up slowly, letting the horse see what she was doing. He looked wary but stood still, allowing her to stroke his nose and cheek. "There, that's not so bad, is it?" she said.

"Looks like you two are hitting it off," Lisa commented.

Carole shrugged. "You know me."

"We *know*, we *know*," Stevie said. "You never met a horse you didn't like."

Carole grinned and reached up to give Ditto a friendly good-bye slap on the neck. To her amazement, the horse threw up his head, snorted, and retreated once again to the back of the stall.

32

Stevie raised one eyebrow. "Hmmm. Maybe we've just found a horse who doesn't like *you*," she teased.

"Don't be ridiculous," Carole said, forcing herself to laugh. It seemed that Ditto was even more skittish than she had thought—quite a change from calm, steady, reliable Starlight. "Just give him a chance. He'll learn to love me."

"HE'S NOTHING LIKE Starlight, that's for sure," Carole said. She was still thinking about her first encounter with Ditto.

Stevie shoved a forkful of coleslaw into her mouth before responding. The three girls were in the crowded mess hall, eating lunch. "You never know," Stevie said at last. "He'll loosen up in a day or two. The first day of camp is a stressful time for the horses."

Carole nodded. "I hope you're right. What do you think, Lisa?"

Carole had to ask the question twice more before Lisa heard her. "Oh! Sorry," she said when she finally started paying attention. "I guess I was thinking about something else."

"Must have been something important," Stevie commented. She pointed at Lisa's plate with her fork. "You've hardly touched your potato chips. Does that mean you don't want them?"

"Help yourself," Lisa said. As Stevie started munching on the potato chips, Lisa leaned her elbows on the table. "I was just trying to figure out how much reading I'll have to do every day to finish all the books I brought." She shook her head and smiled. "But to answer your question, Carole, I don't think you have to worry about Ditto. I'm sure you'll get along fine once you get to know each other."

Stevie licked salt off her fingers and looked around the room. "I can't believe Phil isn't here yet," she said. "If it weren't for Teddy, I'd think he wasn't even at camp."

Just then two boys entered the mess hall, skateboards tucked under their arms. "There he is," Carole said, pointing to one of the boys.

Stevie's eyes lit up. "It's about time," she said. She frowned. "What's he doing with that skateboard? I didn't know he even had one." She didn't wait for an answer but hopped out of her seat. "I'd better go say hi. I'm sure he's been looking for me, too. We probably just missed each other."

But before she could go, Barry walked to the front of the room and called for attention. "Welcome, Moose Hill campers," he said. "I hope you're enjoying your lunch. I have a few announcements to make."

Stevie sat down again, casting a wistful glance at Phil, who was sitting with the other boy at a table near the door. Then she turned her attention to Barry.

"For those of you visiting us for the first time, my name is Barry and I'm the camp director," he said. "My office is in the rec hall, and the door is always open. You can come to me with questions, comments, complaints, and especially compliments." There was a ripple of laughter from the campers. "But seriously," Barry went on, "if you have any problems here, just let me know and I'll do my best to help."

Carole and Lisa exchanged glances. This sounded like the old Barry. So why hadn't he tried harder to help them?

Barry continued. "For you veterans out there, I'm sure you'll notice that we've made some changes here since last year. There are more cabins, for one thing—almost twice as many. But there aren't just more campers here now, there are more things to do as well. We've put in tennis courts and set up volleyball nets at the west end of the meadow. There's also a new arts and crafts studio in the rec hall for you artistic types. I hope everyone will check it out." He paused to take a sip of water. "As the old-timers know, we always have a horse show at the end of camp to show off our newly honed riding skills."

There was an excited murmur from the crowd at that one. Lisa glanced around the room. Twice as many campers meant twice as much competition for ribbons.

"In addition," Barry said, "we're going to have a different kind of show at the end of the first two weeks. But not a horse show. This one will be a talent show. I'd like to ask each cabin to put together some kind of skit or performance for it."

Stevie grinned. A talent show? It sounded fun—that sort of thing was right up her alley. With her creative mind helping them, her cabin was sure to have the best skit in the entire camp. She glanced at Carole, who grinned back at her. Stevie could tell she was thinking the same thing.

Then both girls looked over at Lisa, and their grins faded as they remembered that she was in a different cabin and wouldn't be a part of their performance. That made the whole thing suddenly seem like less fun.

Barry glanced at his watch. "Anyway, I guess that's about it from me," he said. "I hope you're all ready for a month of hard riding and good times. Enjoy your lunch." He gave a wave and then left the room.

"Great," Stevie said. She grabbed the last of her sandwich and shoved it into her mouth. "With all these changes, I'm glad the good food hasn't changed a bit," she mumbled as she chewed. Then she got up and hurried toward Phil.

Carole was thinking about Barry's announcements, too. "You know, I'm glad Starlight will be here for the last two weeks instead of the first two," she told Lisa. "That way I'll get to ride him in the big show. I'm sure I'll do a lot better on him than I would on Ditto."

"You'd do great on any horse," Lisa said, taking a sip of juice.

Carole sighed. "I'm not so sure about that," she said. "I have a bad feeling about Ditto."

Lisa looked surprised. "But you just met him. Don't tell me you've already made up your mind."

"I guess not," Carole said. "I'm just a little worried, that's all."

Lisa patted her friend's hand. "I'm not worried. I know you'll be fine. Have you forgotten what Max says? A good rider can ride any horse well. And you're not just a good rider—you're better than good."

Carole smiled a little. Lisa's encouraging words were making her feel better. "You're right," she said. "I guess I'm just feeling weird because I miss Starlight. But I know I'll like Ditto almost as much."

"That's the spirit." Lisa drained her juice glass, then

stood up. "Come on, are you finished? We should get over to the stable and tack up for our first class." Staff members had passed out schedules as the campers had walked into the mess hall. Carole, Stevie, and Lisa were all in the same jump class after lunch.

"I'm ready," Carole said. She and Lisa hurried over to Phil's table. Stevie was chattering at her boyfriend a mile a minute, and it took some doing to drag her away. But finally she got up and joined her friends.

"I was right. That wasn't Phil's skateboard," she said as the three girls walked to the stable. "It belongs to his cabin mate Todd—that's the guy he came in with. He's a skateboard nut. He brought not one, not two, but *three* skateboards to camp with him. Can you believe that?"

"No," said Lisa, remembering the unpaved road leading to the camp. "Especially since the only place to skateboard around here must be the new tennis courts."

"That's where they were before lunch," Stevie said. "That's why I couldn't find Phil. But Todd also wants to try boarding on the delivery ramp behind the kitchen." She rolled her eyes. "Boy, I'll bet Phil is glad I'm here. Otherwise he'd be forced to spend all his time hanging around with the skateboard fiend. What a bore."

By now the girls had reached the stable. They headed first for the tack room, which was crowded with other campers. Carole found Ditto's tack quickly. As she picked it up, she noticed that there were no stable hands among the campers in the room. That was surprising. Usually at least half the riders sat back and let the staff tack up for them.

Carole left the tack room and hurried to Ditto's stall. After Lisa's pep talk, she was eager to really get acquainted with her temporary mount. If she saddled up quickly, she should have a few minutes alone in the ring with him. Fortunately he seemed a little calmer than he had been earlier, and he didn't object to the quick grooming she gave him.

He took the bridle easily, though he chomped on the bit for a few seconds before letting go. Carole hoisted the saddle and did her best to place it on his back gently, remembering his jumpiness that morning. But he didn't react until she started tightening the girth. Then he suddenly danced sideways to the end of his lead, causing Carole accidentally to yank on the girth and pull the saddle off-kilter.

She took a deep breath. "All right, boy," she said calmly. "Settle down. I guess you don't like a tight girth, huh? I'll have to keep that in mind." After tightening the girth as much as the horse would allow, she unclipped his lead line and led him outside. She could tighten the girth the rest of the way once she was in the saddle. Starlight didn't mind having the girth tightened, but Carole had ridden plenty of horses that did.

When Carole and Ditto reached the ring, it was empty. "Good," she said. "That will give us a chance to get used to each other before class starts." She led Ditto to the mounting block and swung herself onto his back. He shifted uneasily under her weight, but he didn't move.

"That's more like it," she said. Leaning over, she quickly tightened the girth and adjusted her stirrups. Then she picked up the reins and signaled for a walk.

Ditto didn't move. Carole signaled again, more firmly this time. At last Ditto seemed to realize what she wanted. He moved off jerkily, his head weaving from side to side. Remembering Betty's comment about Ditto having a mind of his own, Carole decided she'd better keep a firm hand. She tightened up on the reins and signaled lightly with her heel for a trot. Ditto shook his head and came to a stop.

Carole bit her lip. What was wrong with this horse? She had given such clear signals that Starlight or any other horse at Pine Hollow would have known instantly what he was supposed to do.

"Come on, boy," she said, leaning over to pat him on the neck. "What's the matter?"

41

Ditto jumped to one side and snorted. Obviously he was still skittish. Carole hoped it wasn't a permanent state, thinking longingly of friendly, steady Starlight. Just then Ditto shook his head violently and took a step backward, snorting suspiciously at a bird that had just landed nearby. Carole tightened up again on the reins, reminding the horse that she was in charge. Why was he so jumpy? To her surprise, she found herself getting annoyed with him. That wasn't like her. She knew horses could be as individual as people, with their own fears, foibles, and personality flaws.

She signaled for a trot again, vowing to be more patient. After a couple of tries Ditto got the message and started trotting. Like many horses, he had a choppy, uneven trot that was hard to ride without posting. Carole clenched her teeth and started to post, thinking longingly of Starlight's smooth, easy trot—one of the first things she had loved about him. Ditto was going to take some getting used to.

SOON THE REST of the class joined Carole and Ditto in the ring. Before starting the lesson, Betty said she had a couple of announcements to make.

"Actually, Barry was supposed to make them at lunch," the instructor said. "I guess they slipped his mind. The first one has to do with the staff here. I'm sure you've already noticed that we don't have many stable hands this year. Those of you who've been with us before may remember that the hands did a lot of your work for you. I hate to be the one to break it to you, but this year you're going to have to do most of your own work. That means grooming, taking care of your tack, and cooling down your horse after you ride. In addition, we'd appreciate it if you all would pitch in occasionally and help with some of the other stable chores, like mucking out stalls and so forth."

There were a few scattered groans, but most of the campers were nodding agreeably. The Saddle Club girls exchanged amused glances. They were all thinking the same thing: Did Max Regnery have anything to do with this? Betty's announcement made Carole wonder about the higher prices, though. Why would it cost more to go to a camp with fewer employees?

Betty wasn't finished. "Okay. Even if you didn't like that news, I think you're all going to like what I have to say next. It's about the end-of-camp horse show. The show will be a little bit different this year."

The Saddle Club exchanged glances again. More changes?

"We came up with something special to try this year," Betty went on. "In addition to the usual events— dressage, equitation, hunter jumping—we're adding an optional event: show jumping."

Carole couldn't believe her ears. Show jumping was an exciting event in which horses and riders competed over a course of jumps in a set period of time. After each competitor completed the course once, there was a jump-off to break any ties. In the jump-off, which was usually the most exciting part of the event for spectators, the jumpers had to go through a shortened version of the course, and if there was a tie, the horse with the fastest time won. As opposed to hunter jumping, in which an even pace, good manners, and sometimes conformation counted for a lot, the only thing that counted in show jumping was to jump the course fast and clean. Carole and her friends had seen show-jumping competitions at horse shows and on television, but none of them had ever taken part in one. Carole was happier than ever that she would be riding Starlight in the show instead of Ditto. She and Starlight were a winning team, and she knew they would do well.

Stevie was excited at the thought of entering, too. Belle's specialty was dressage, but she was also a strong and fast jumper. Stevie couldn't wait to try her out over a real show-jumping course.

Lisa had always been a good jumper, but she knew show jumping was a strenuous event. She decided to wait to see how things went with Major before she made up her mind whether or not to give it a try.

"Nobody should feel pressured to enter this part of the show," Betty said, as if reading Lisa's mind. "It's a tough event, and not everyone will be ready for it. But you'll have plenty of time to think it over before you decide.

"Okay, that's enough talking for now. Let's ride!"

For the rest of the class, Stevie and Lisa thought about Betty's exciting news during every spare moment. But for Carole, there were no spare moments. Even when just standing still, Ditto kept her busy. If she relaxed her attention for even a second, he would take a step or lower his head or do something else he wasn't supposed to do. Besides that, she was having trouble communicating with him. Several times during the class, Carole thought she was finally getting through to him. But as soon as she began to relax and enjoy herself, Ditto would surprise her by ignoring or misinterpreting her commands once again. Even Betty noticed that Carole was having trouble.

"Are you okay?" the instructor asked at one point, riding up to Carole and speaking quietly so the other campers wouldn't overhear. "You seem to be having trouble with Ditto."

"Don't worry," Carole said quickly, blushing a little. "We're still getting to know each other. I'm sure he'll be fine by tomorrow."

Betty nodded and rode away. The instructor had believed Carole's words. So why didn't Carole believe them herself?

AT THE END of class, Betty made one more announcement. "In the spirit of friendly competition, I decided to make things a little more interesting in this class," she said. "At the end of each day, I'll be awarding a prize to the rider who I think has done the best that day. This is a completely subjective decision, based only on my own opinion about who's worked hardest or learned the most. So it pays to do your best, pay attention, and ask questions. Got it?"

The students nodded. Lisa smiled to herself. She was always winning this kind of prize at school. Teachers liked her, and she liked to do her best. Judging by Betty's words, doing your best was more important to this prize than being the best rider.

"Good," Betty said. She dug into the pocket of her jacket and pulled something out. "Since I'm a little short of gold trophies, the prize will be this candy bar. It's wrapped in gold foil—I hope that's close enough. And I'm happy to announce that our very first gold-candy-bar winner is . . . Stevie Lake!"

Stevie grinned and rode forward to collect her prize. Carole started to applaud but had to stop when Ditto took the opportunity to toss his head and dance sideways. Luckily the rest of the class took over, clapping politely.

Lisa clapped along with the rest, but her heart wasn't really in it. It didn't seem quite fair for Stevie to win. After all, she was riding her own horse, while most of the others in the class were on camp horses. Of course that gave her an advantage. Didn't Betty realize that?

The campers dismounted and started to lead their horses inside. Stevie caught up with Carole and Lisa, grinning ear to ear. "How about that, huh?" she said, holding up her candy bar. "I bet you never would have picked me for the teacher's pet."

Carole laughed. She was still feeling bad about her performance with Ditto that day, but she was happy for her friend. Stevie had done well, and she deserved the prize. "I know why you won," she teased. "You were so busy plotting how you're going to win a blue ribbon in show jumping that you forgot to goof off in class."

"Well, maybe," Stevie conceded with a wink. "Anybody hungry? I'll split my prize with you. We're one for all and all for one, right? Even when it comes to chocolate."

"Thanks anyway," Carole said. "But I'm still stuffed from lunch. Even if I weren't, that class would have made me lose my appetite. If I'm going to be riding Ditto for the next two weeks, I'll have to figure out a better way to deal with him. He was a mess today."

"You'll do it," Stevie said confidently. "You're the pride of Pine Hollow Stables, remember? No horse alive stands a chance against you." She turned to Lisa and held out the candy bar invitingly. "How about you? I know you must be hungry, since I ate all your potato chips."

But Lisa shook her head. "No thanks," she said. She *was* a little hungry, but the last thing in the world she wanted was to eat somebody else's prize. She would just have to work harder in class from now on so she could win some candy bars of her own.

Stevie shrugged. "Okay," she said. "More for me." Suddenly her eyes lit up. "Actually, make that more for me and Phil. We have a flat class together next."

"Lisa and I have a horsemanship lecture now," Carole said. "I guess we'll see you later."

"Bye," Stevie said. She led Belle toward the water trough as her friends went inside to untack their horses.

A few minutes later, Carole and Lisa were seated in the main room of the rec hall for the unmounted horsemanship course, which would cover all aspects of horse care and stable management. The instructor hadn't arrived yet, and other students were still trickling in. Piper Sullivan entered and saw Lisa and Carole.

"Hi," she said, walking over to them. "Mind if I join you?" Lisa scooted aside to make room, and the older girl sat down next to her. "Whew! I'm glad the class hasn't started yet," Piper said. "I had to untack

Tap after our last class, and I was sure I was going to be late."

"You had cross-country class before this, right?" Carole asked.

Piper nodded. "How did you know that?"

"I saw your class riding in while I was cooling down Ditto after our jump class," Carole explained. "You and Tapestry look really terrific together—you really seem to be in synch." *Not like me and Ditto*, she added silently to herself.

"Thanks," Piper said. She stared down at her hands, as if uncomfortable with the compliment. "I owe it all to Tap. She's a really great horse."

Lisa had seen Piper ride in, too, and she thought the older girl was being too modest. It was clear that Piper knew what she was doing in the saddle. She had guided Tapestry without seeming to move while she did it. "You and Tap must be awfully good at dressage," she said, continuing the thought aloud.

"Not really," Piper said. "I mean, Tap is talented enough to do it, but I don't have as much time to work with her as I'd like, what with schoolwork and other stuff."

Lisa nodded. She understood that feeling very well. She couldn't count how many times she had had to cut her time at the stable short because she had homework to do or dance or art lessons to attend.

"What school do you go to?" Carole asked.

"Willoughby Prep," Piper answered. "It's in Maryland."

"Wow," Lisa said, impressed. Willoughby was a prestigious boarding school with a great academic reputation. Many of the students there were accepted at the top universities in the country.

Piper shrugged. "I'm just a day student. My family lives right down the road from the school."

"Still, it must be tough to keep up there," Lisa said. If she was worried about doing well at Willow Creek Junior High School, she couldn't even imagine how much pressure she would feel at a place like Willoughby.

"It's no big deal," Piper said, pushing her shoulder-length hair out of her face. "It's just a school. But it helps to come from there if you want to get into a good college."

Carole was much more interested in talking about riding than about where people went to school. "So, have you had Tapestry long?" she asked.

"About a year and a half," Piper said, shifting to a more comfortable position. "She was a gift from my parents."

"A Christmas present?" Carole asked, remembering the Christmas when her father had surprised her by giving her Starlight.

"No," Piper replied without further explanation. "What about you two? How long have you been riding?"

Carole could tell that Piper was trying to change the subject, but she didn't mind. Maybe her family was rich enough to buy her a horse for no occasion at all, and she didn't want to sound as though she was bragging. "I've been riding since I was four," Carole said quickly, hoping she hadn't already embarrassed the other girl. "Lisa hasn't been riding as long as me and Stevie and some of the other intermediate riders at our stable, but she's really catching up."

Lisa gave Carole a surprised look. Was that really what her friends thought of her riding ability? Maybe she wasn't yet as skilled as Carole and Stevie, but she had thought she was good enough to be considered as another member of the intermediate class at Pine Hollow, not as someone who was still trying to catch up.

She glanced at Piper, hoping her cabin mate wouldn't think she was a hopeless beginner because of Carole's comment. But Piper and Carole were both looking at the door as the instructor entered the room.

Good, Lisa thought. *Maybe Piper didn't hear.* It was clear that riding and schoolwork both came easily to

Piper, so easily that she seemed surprised when people complimented her on them. Lisa wanted to be like that someday. She wanted to be good at things without having to struggle, to be able to take good grades and intermediate riding for granted. In the meantime, she still had to work for everything she got. But she would keep on working, waiting for the moment when it all came together and she was as good as she could be at school, riding, everything. Just like Piper.

6

"I CAN'T BELIEVE Phil is going skateboarding *again*." Stevie glared across the meadow. Phil and Todd were just disappearing behind the trees that hid the tennis courts from view.

It was Tuesday afternoon. The last riding class of the day had just ended and the campers had an hour and a half of free time before dinner. The Saddle Club's horses were back in their stalls, freshly groomed. The three girls had been filling their water buckets at the outdoor spigot when Stevie had spotted Phil hurrying off with Todd, skateboard in hand. She had called out to him, planning to invite him to come to the arts and crafts room with them. But Phil had just waved and continued on his way, not even waiting to hear what she wanted.

"Try not to think about it, Stevie," Lisa suggested with a sigh. She rubbed her eyes, which were red and sore.

"Are you okay?" Carole asked Lisa. "You don't look so good."

Lisa stifled a yawn. She had stayed up reading *The Old Man and the Sea* after lights-out the evening before, using a flashlight under her blanket. It was the second book of the twenty she was supposed to read. "I'm okay," she said. But as she remembered how many books she still had to go, she felt an anxious knot form in the pit of her stomach. "Just a little tired. Maybe I'll just head back to the cabin now and do some reading."

"No, you don't," Stevie said, turning away from Phil long enough to respond. "We're going to try out the new arts and crafts room before dinner, remember?"

"But I want to get started on *The Great Gatsby*, and—" Lisa began.

Stevie cut her off. "Forget it," she said firmly. "We haven't had a real Saddle Club meeting since camp started, and we're overdue for one." She glanced toward the tennis courts again. "It just so happens I have a little problem I need some advice about."

Reluctantly, Lisa agreed. As soon as they had put the

water buckets in their horses' stalls, the three girls headed to the rec hall. As they walked there, Lisa kept glancing at her watch. But as soon as she entered the large, light-filled arts and crafts room, her eyes lit up.

"Hey, look!" she exclaimed. "There's a pottery wheel!" Lisa had used a pottery wheel in an art class once. "And nobody's using it." She gave her friends an eager glance. "Do you guys mind if I grab it?"

"No problem," Carole said, smiling at Lisa's enthusiasm. She looked around at the other art supplies, which were stacked on the open shelves that lined two walls of the room. "I think I'll try some of that modeling clay. Maybe I can make a sculpture of Starlight so I won't miss him so much."

"Sculpting sounds like fun," Stevie said. "Get some clay down for me, too, okay?" Soon she and Carole were settled at a table near the pottery wheel.

A few other campers were also in the room, but all of them were concentrating on their own work, and the place was quiet. That made it easy for The Saddle Club to talk as they worked.

"So, Stevie, about this problem of yours . . . ," Carole began.

Stevie didn't need any more of an invitation. "I can't believe the way he's acting!" she exclaimed. "Before we got here, he was gung ho about hanging out together,

56

but he seems to have forgotten all about that. Half the time he doesn't even remember I'm here." Stevie looked down and realized that she was squeezing her clay so hard that she had obliterated all signs of the head she was trying to sculpt. She rolled the clay into a ball and started re-forming the nose.

"Maybe he's still getting used to his new cabin mates and his riding classes and stuff," Carole suggested.

"So am I," Stevie pointed out. "And I still have enough time left over to spend with him. At least I would if he were ever around."

Lisa smoothed the sides of the graceful vase that was forming between her hands. "I think Carole has a point," she said. "There's an awful lot to do here, and hardly enough hours in the day to get it all done."

"He might have a little more time to spend with me if he didn't waste so much skateboarding . . . ," Stevie began. Just then her gaze fell on Carole's clay. Her voice trailed off, and she started to laugh. "What is *that* supposed to be?"

Carole looked at her piece. She couldn't help laughing, too. Despite her best efforts, her sculpture of Starlight resembled nothing so much as a huge, lopsided pinecone with legs. "What do you mean? It's a masterpiece." She glanced at Lisa's clay. "How do you do it, Lisa? Your vase looks great."

57

Lisa stopped her wheel and gave her piece a critical look. "Not really," she said. "It's crooked, see?"

"It doesn't look crooked to me," Stevie said.

But Lisa crushed the vase back into a ball. "I'd better start over," she said. Within moments, another slender vase was taking shape under her skilled hands.

Stevie shrugged. She hadn't seen anything wrong with the first vase, but she knew Lisa was a perfectionist. She turned her attention back to Carole. "Don't take this the wrong way, but I think all your hand-eye coordination must be dedicated to your riding," she said, as Carole tried to reshape Starlight's head. Or was it his tail? Stevie couldn't tell. "It's a good thing you're a better rider than sculptor—for Starlight's sake, that is."

"Please, don't mention Starlight and riding in the same sentence," Carole replied. "You'll just remind me of how much I miss having him here. The real him, that is." She gazed at her clay and sighed.

"You and Ditto still aren't getting along, huh?" Stevie said. She stuck a couple of pieces of clay onto her piece to form a mouth. They looked more like a pair of wilting string beans than human lips, but she liked the effect, so she decided to leave them exactly as they were.

"That's an understatement. Every time I think I'm making progress, he does something wrong again. Half

58

the time he doesn't even seem to understand my aids." Carole sighed again. "It's such a big change from Starlight—he's always so responsive. Even when he doesn't understand exactly what I'm asking of him, he always tries his hardest."

"I'm sure you can get through to Ditto if you just keep trying," Lisa said. "Where there's a will, there's a way."

"I'm just not sure I have the will this time," Carole said, frowning. "I wish I'd never let Max talk me into this stupid plan. I miss my horse."

"So I guess we're all missing someone right about now," Lisa commented, smoothing the sides of her new vase. "You miss Starlight, Stevie misses Phil, and I miss you guys."

Carole gasped, at the same time accidentally demolishing three of her sculpture's legs. "Oh, Lisa!" she exclaimed. "I'm sorry. We haven't even asked you how it's going in Cabin Six. Are you completely miserable?"

"It's actually not that bad," Lisa said. "I mean, I see you guys during the day, and at night I mostly concentrate on my reading. Besides, the other girls in my cabin are pretty nice. Especially Piper. She's terrific—she's really got it all together."

Carole nodded as she reshaped her clay. "She's a wonderful rider," she said. "She's in my equitation class, and it's a good thing there's no candy-bar prize there. If there was, she'd embarrass the rest of us by winning it every day. That mare of hers never puts a foot wrong."

"I've noticed," Stevie said, carefully arranging long, spaghetti-like pieces of clay on her sculpture's head to form hair. "We'd better watch out, or the two of them will ride off with all the blue ribbons at the horse show."

"Don't count on it," Carole said with a grin. "I'll be back on Starlight by then, remember? We'll give them a run for their money—especially in the show-jumping event."

"Does that mean you've decided to enter?" Lisa asked.

"Definitely," Carole replied. "I think it's going to be really exciting. What about you, Stevie?"

Stevie nodded. "I think so, as long as Belle seems ready. I don't want to push her too hard, but I'm dying to enter."

"I'm sure she'll be ready," Carole said, trying to raise one of her clay horse's legs to make him look as if he were prancing. In the process, she accidentally squashed his head. She did her best to fix it as she continued to talk. "You've got her in really good shape, and she's so naturally athletic. She'll probably have a ball."

Lisa cleared her throat. "I was thinking about maybe entering, too," she said shyly. In the past couple of days, she had realized what a strong jumper Major was. On his back, she was sure she could at least avoid embarrassing herself. And riding in the event would be a great experience.

Carole and Stevie looked surprised. "Really?" Carole asked immediately. "Do you think you're ready for that?"

She regretted her thoughtless words immediately when she saw Lisa's face fall.

"Sorry, I didn't mean it that way," Carole said, abandoning her sculpture and turning to Lisa. "I just meant you don't have to decide yet if you don't want to."

But Lisa knew what Carole was really thinking—that Lisa wasn't good enough for that kind of event yet. Stevie was thinking the same thing. Lisa could tell by the look on her face. What made them think they were still so much more advanced than her? Lisa was getting a little tired of always being automatically labeled the weakest rider of the three. Maybe this was as good a time as any to prove that she wasn't their inferior anymore.

"I've already decided," she said firmly. "I *am* going to enter that show jumping event. And you'd better watch out, because I just might surprise everybody and win!"

She switched off the pottery wheel. The vase she had been making was pretty good, but the rim was definitely uneven. Lisa smashed the clay down into a ball and put it away.

"What are you doing?" Stevie asked.

"I've had enough arts and crafts for now," Lisa replied. "I'm going back to my cabin. See you later."

Carole watched her go. "Whew," she said. "I guess I put my foot in my mouth that time."

"Don't worry," Stevie said. "She's probably just dying to get back to *War and Peace* or whatever she's reading now."

"*The Great Gatsby*," Carole corrected. She frowned anxiously. "I hope that's it. She seemed kind of insulted by what I said."

"She'll get over it," Stevie said. "She's probably just tired and hungry. It's been a long day."

"I guess you're right," Carole said.

By this time, most of the other campers had left to go to dinner. The arts and crafts room was almost deserted.

"Come on," Stevie said. "I'm just about done with this." She sat back and gave her sculpture a critical look. Most people would probably recognize it as a human head, but beyond that it was rather difficult to describe. The nose tapered almost to a point, one ear was a little higher than the other, and several pieces of hair had fallen off, leaving blank patches on the head.

Carole looked at it and laughed. "Who's that supposed to be?"

"It started off as a self-portrait," Stevie admitted with

62

a grin. "But if you tell anyone I said that, I'll deny it. Even my last school picture was more flattering."

"Well, I'm the last one to make fun of you," Carole said, gesturing at her own sculpture. "Still, even if nobody else can tell it's a horse, *I* know it's supposed to be Starlight. And that's all that matters." She carefully picked up the sculpture and carried it over to an empty shelf to dry.

"Right," Stevie said. "And if anybody asks, you can just tell them it's an abstract modernist piece and they obviously just don't get it." She picked up her own creation and set it next to Carole's. "Normally I would give this masterpiece to Phil, but right now I'm not sure he deserves it. I think I'll give it to my parents. They won't mind if it's a little strange-looking. After all, they hang every one of my darling little brother Michael's hideous space warrior pictures on the refrigerator."

The two girls cleaned up the table where they had been working and then washed their hands in the sink. Carole rubbed her stomach. "All that creating made me hungry," she said. "Let's go to dinner."

"Sounds good to me," Stevie said. She paused on the threshold and glanced at their sculptures, sitting side by side on the shelf. "But you know what? I don't think our cabin should do a sculpting demonstration for the talent show."

* * *

WHEN LISA ARRIVED at Cabin Six, Piper was the only one there. She was wearing sweatpants and a T-shirt, and her hair was tied back in a ponytail.

"Hi," Piper said when Lisa entered. "I was just about to go for a run. Want to come?" She began to stretch.

Lisa flopped onto her bunk. "No thanks," she said. "I hate jogging. Don't tell my dance teacher, though. She's always trying to convince me I should run every day."

"You take dance?" Piper asked, looking interested. "What kind?"

"Ballet," Lisa replied. "I've been taking classes for almost five years now. Other than the jogging stuff, I really like it."

Piper turned the stretch she was doing into a plié. "I used to take ballet, too," she said. "All through elementary school. Now I take a modern dance class three times a week."

"Really?" Suddenly Lisa sat up. "Hey, that gives me a great idea. Why don't we do a dance number for the talent show?"

"That's perfect!" Piper said, stopping her stretching long enough to clap her hands and smile. "I was afraid we'd end up just doing some kind of embarrassingly silly skit or something. But with the two of us working to-

64

gether, we should be able to come up with a really great number."

Lisa reached into the cubby next to her bunk for a pencil and paper. "Come on," she said excitedly. "Let's start writing down some ideas. The other girls in the cabin probably don't have much dance experience, so we'll want to start rehearsals as soon as we can."

Piper stopped stretching and sat down next to her. "How about making it a sort of modern jazz piece?" she suggested. "I know Betty is a jazz fan. I'm sure she'd let us borrow her boom box and one of her tapes."

"That sounds really great," Lisa agreed. She had never tried jazz dancing, but she had seen other people do it and she was sure she could do it if she rehearsed enough. It seemed like fun.

"We should be sure to pick a fast song," Piper said. "That way we can have lots of cool kicks and flashy moves and jumps in the choreography. Like this, maybe." She stood and executed a graceful leap across the cabin floor.

Lisa clapped. "That was great!" she cried. "If we all do that in unison, it will look fantastic." For the next fifteen minutes, the two girls were busy writing down ideas.

Finally Lisa paused and glanced at her watch. "This all sounds perfect so far," she said. "What do you say we take a break and go to dinner? Maybe we can talk more about it there."

"You go ahead," Piper said. She stood up and did a few more stretches. "I still want to get that run in."

"But you'll miss dinner," Lisa protested.

Piper shrugged. "It's okay," she said. "I had a huge lunch. I'm not even hungry right now. I can grab something from the snack machine in the rec hall if I get hungry later." With a wave, she hurried out of the cabin. Lisa heard her sneakers pounding down the path toward the woods.

Lisa stood up to put away the pencil and paper. Piper had self-discipline, that was for sure. Lisa couldn't help admiring the older girl even more. She glanced at the open bag of books beside her bunk and sighed. She could use a little more of that kind of discipline herself.

Suddenly she decided there was no reason she couldn't at least try to follow Piper's example. "If she can do it, so can I," she murmured. Skipping one meal was a good idea anyway. She could stand to lose a couple of pounds no matter what anybody else said. And if she could lose the weight then she could do anything—and it would all be as easy for her as it was for Piper.

She sat down again on her bunk and picked up *The*

Great Gatsby, willing herself to ignore her grumbling stomach. Opening to the first chapter, she started to read.

"I HOPE SHE'S not mad at me," Carole said worriedly. She and Stevie were almost finished with their dinners, and Lisa still hadn't shown up in the mess hall.

Stevie buttered her third roll. The rolls were still warm from the oven, and they tasted delicious after a strenuous day of riding. "She doesn't know what she's missing," she commented. "These rolls are fantastic. They almost make me forget that a certain someone didn't even try to come sit with us, even though we saved him a seat." Phil was sitting across the room with his cabin mates again.

Carole ignored Stevie's comment. She was still feeling anxious about Lisa. "I wasn't very sensitive when we were talking about the show-jumping event," she said. "Lisa really is a good rider. As her friends, it's our job to remind her how far she's come, not how much farther she has to go. Even though I was surprised she was thinking about riding in the event, I shouldn't have said so."

"What's said is said," Stevie said philosophically, taking a large bite of her roll. After chewing and swallowing, she added, "The only thing we can do is find her and talk to her. If she's mad at you, she's probably mad at me, too. I'm sure I looked just as surprised as you sounded."

"You're right," Carole said, setting down the piece of fried chicken she was holding. "Hurry up and finish eating. Then we'll go to her cabin and apologize."

A few minutes later the two girls knocked gently on the door of Cabin Six. There was no answer, so they pushed the door open and peeked inside. The cabin was dark and empty.

"Now what?" Stevie asked as she and Carole stood on the path in front of the cabin. It was a cloudy evening, and the woods seemed darker than usual. "She wasn't at dinner; she's not in the cabin. Where is she?"

"Maybe she went for a swim," Carole suggested. "Let's go down to the pond and—"

Suddenly Stevie held up her hand. "Shhh. Did you hear that?"

"Hear what?"

Stevie listened carefully for a moment. The sound came again—the sound of something or someone moving through the woods somewhere behind Cabin Six. "That!"

"Maybe it's Lisa," Carole said. "Maybe she went for a walk and she's just getting back. Come on, let's go see." She started around the side of the cabin. The underbrush

68

was creeping up on the structure, and it wasn't easy getting through in some spots.

Stevie kicked a dead branch out of the way. "This isn't exactly the ideal terrain for a walk." She looked ahead and caught a glimpse of something moving through the trees about a dozen yards away from them. She squinted, trying to see more clearly in the dusky dimness of the forest. "Did you see that?"

"What?" Carole asked, looking up from the vine she was untangling from around her leg. She was glad it wasn't poison ivy.

But by the time Stevie pointed it out, the shape was gone. "It wasn't Lisa, anyway," she said. "Too big. It sort of looked like a man in dark clothes—like maybe in a business suit."

Carole looked skeptical. "What would a businessman be doing out there in the woods?"

"Who knows?" Stevie said. "For all we know, he could be an ax murderer or something. Maybe we should report it."

Now Carole looked suspicious. "Oh, really?" she said. "The more I think about it, the more this seems like a Stevie Lake prank to me. Are you sure you're not just trying to trick me into reporting something ridiculous and making a fool of myself in front of Barry?"

"Of course not," Stevie said, sounding wounded. "I

really did see someone. Or something. Maybe it was a bear."

"A bear? In a business suit?" Carole said.

Stevie sighed. "Come on," she said, fighting her way back through the weeds and vines to the front of the cabin. "Let's keep looking for Lisa. I bet she's at the pond."

The two girls walked down to the swimming pond. Sure enough, Lisa was there. She waved at her friends and swam to the shallows by the small beach.

"We've been looking everywhere for you," Stevie said. "We missed you at dinner."

Lisa squeezed some water out of her hair. "I wasn't really hungry," she said. That wasn't exactly true, but she did feel a lot better now that she had finished several chapters of her book. "I just came down here to cool off. Why don't you come in?"

Carole was glad that Lisa didn't seem angry. "We'd better not right now," she said. "We should let our dinners settle. But I did want to talk to you. I'm sorry about what I said earlier—there's no reason you shouldn't be in the show-jumping competition."

"No need to apologize," Lisa said with a shrug. "I know you meant well." Her earlier anger had passed. After all, her friends would realize how wrong they were

70

soon enough. There was no sense in making a big deal about it in the meantime.

Stevie looked up at the sound of a door swinging shut on one of the boys' cabins across the pond. "Hey, there's Phil," she said. Then she frowned. "Ugh. He's with Todd. At least they don't have those stupid skateboards with them for a change." She grabbed Carole's arm. "Come on, let's go say hi. Maybe you can distract Todd long enough for me to talk to Phil for a few minutes." She was only half joking. "Want to come, Lisa?"

"You guys go ahead," Lisa said. "I just got in the water—I want to swim for a while."

"All right," Carole said. As Lisa backstroked out to the middle of the pond, Carole and Stevie hurried around it and caught up with the two boys.

"Hi, Phil," Stevie greeted her boyfriend sweetly. She glanced at Todd. "Hi, Todd," she added in a much less enthusiastic voice. "What are you two up to?"

"We were just going to play tennis," Phil said.

"Where are your rackets?" Carole asked, noticing that the boys were empty-handed.

Todd gave her a strange look. "We're going to use the camp rackets," he said. "We didn't bring our own."

Phil laughed. "Don't mind Carole," he told his new friend. "If I know her, she's probably spent every minute since she got here at the stable. I'm surprised she even knew the tennis courts existed, let alone the equipment shed."

Carole blushed. It was true that she had been spending a lot of time at the stable, even if she hadn't been enjoying it as much as usual, thanks to Ditto. "You got me," she admitted. "I haven't quite made it down to the courts yet."

"Why don't we go check them out now?" Stevie suggested brightly. She turned to Phil. "How about it? Are you up for a game of doubles?" She smiled as she pictured herself as Phil's teammate, winning point after point from Carole and Todd until they gave in and begged for mercy. Now *that* was what she called romantic.

"Sure," Phil said, smiling at Stevie. "Is that okay with you, Todd?"

Todd grinned. "On one condition," he said. "Boys against girls!"

Phil laughed. "Good idea," he said. "How about it, Stevie? Carole? Unless you think you can't possibly beat us, of course . . ."

There was no way Stevie could resist a challenge like that, especially from Phil. "You're on," she said grimly. Without another word, she stalked off toward the courts.

Carole tried not to giggle as she hurried after Stevie

72

and the two boys. This had the makings of an interesting game, she thought. She and Stevie were both pretty good players, and they would definitely give the boys a run for their money—especially considering the mood Stevie was in. Carole gladly banished from her mind all thoughts of the silly misunderstanding with Lisa and the much more serious misunderstanding with Ditto. *This* was what camp was really all about—having fun.

CAROLE DIDN'T HAVE much fun for the next couple of days. Her relationship with Ditto wasn't getting better over time. If anything, it was getting even worse. She was starting to do something she never thought she'd do: lose patience with a horse. Every time Ditto misconstrued a simple command or ignored an aid, Carole regretted ever saying that she'd never met a horse she didn't like. She had met one now, that was for sure. Several times during the week she had even thought about asking Barry to switch her to another horse. But her pride overcame that thought each time. She had never met a horse she couldn't ride, and she wasn't about to let Ditto break her streak.

On the other hand, she had so much trouble controlling him that it was hard for her to pay attention in her riding classes. So far, she hadn't won the candy bar a single time in jump class. In her equitation and general riding classes, she was lucky to make it through with a minimum of errors.

Worst of all was dressage class. Normally Carole enjoyed dressage, though she wasn't as crazy about it as Stevie was. But normally Carole was riding Starlight, who was a quick learner and eager to please. Ditto was just the opposite, and he absolutely refused to learn anything Carole tried to teach him about the demanding and intricate sport.

In Friday's dressage class, the campers were performing tests that put together all the skills they had been working on that week. As she waited her turn, Carole patted Ditto on the neck, hoping that if she acted as though she liked him, she would convince him—and herself—that she really did. He jumped nervously, and Carole gritted her teeth.

After a moment, Ditto calmed down again. "You're going to do your best, right, boy?" Carole whispered to the horse. He flicked one ear lazily back toward her, then took a step forward and stretched his neck down to nibble at some weeds by the fence.

Carole pulled his head up and, after several tries, got him to step back into place. She turned to watch as Stevie began her test. As usual, both she and Belle seemed to be enjoying themselves, making their good performance look even better. When she finished, Stevie was smiling broadly.

"Nice job," Carole said, as her friend pulled up beside her.

"Thanks," Stevie said breathlessly. "It felt good. Belle is really on today."

Carole grimaced. "I wish I could say the same about Ditto," she grumbled. "He hasn't been on since I've known him."

Stevie gave her a sympathetic look. Then she glanced over to where Piper was getting ready to begin her round on Tapestry. "This should be good," Stevie predicted.

And she was right. Tapestry performed beautifully, hardly taking a wrong step. On her back, Piper sat upright and still. Her aids—the signals she used to tell the horse what to do—were almost completely invisible, just as they should be for dressage.

When the pair finished, Stevie let out a quiet whistle of appreciation. "That was fantastic," she said.

"No kidding. They made it look so easy," Carole said.

"That's what they're supposed to do," Stevie reminded her.

Carole sighed. "I know," she said, as Ditto shifted beneath her. She tightened up on the reins to prevent him from taking another step. "But right now this test seems anything but easy to me."

The instructor called Carole last. "Wish me luck," she told Stevie grimly.

"Good luck," Stevie said. "Or maybe I should say, 'Break a leg.'"

"If only," Carole said, only half joking. "If Ditto really did break his leg, at least I wouldn't have to ride him anymore." She rode to the starting point.

The test was a complete disaster from the beginning. Despite Carole's signal, Ditto started off on the wrong lead, and it was all downhill from there. He veered off course on the center straightaway, refused to heed her signal to turn into a figure eight until they were nearly at the far end of the ring, and slowed to a walk when he was supposed to move into a canter. By the end of the exercise, Carole was fuming. She slid off the horse's back as soon as the instructor dismissed the class and led him inside without a word.

"Hey, wait up," Stevie called after her. She and Belle

caught up to Carole and Ditto just as they entered the stable. "Where are you going? We have a trail class now, remember?"

"I'm not going," Carole said. "I've had it with this horse." She gestured at Ditto, who was pulling at his lead, eager to get back to his stall and his feed trough.

"What do you mean?" Stevie asked.

"I mean I can't take it anymore," Carole said. "Ditto and I just don't get along. I'm going to ask Barry to switch me to another horse." Her pride in her riding had its limit, and she had reached it today.

Stevie looked dubious. "Do you really think he'll do that?" she asked. "He hasn't been exactly helpful lately." As she had promised Lisa, Stevie had tried to talk to Barry about the cabin situation earlier in the week, but she hadn't had any more luck than her friends had. "Why don't we have a Saddle Club meeting at lunch? Maybe we can figure out something else you can try." Lisa wasn't in their dressage or trail classes, so lunch would be the first chance they would have to talk with her.

"Thanks, but no thanks," Carole said stubbornly. "I've already decided what to do. I don't want to be stuck on this uncooperative horse for another whole week."

Carole said good-bye to Stevie, then untacked and groomed Ditto quickly. She refilled his bucket with

78

clean water and cleaned his tack. She would never consider taking less than perfect care of any horse, even if this particular one wasn't exactly her favorite.

Finally everything was done. Carole hurried to the rec hall. Barry wasn't in his office, and his assistant had no idea where he was. Carole had to search half the camp before she finally found him in the grain shed. He had a calculator in his hand and a worried look on his face.

Carole didn't pay attention to either one. "Barry, I've got a big problem," she announced.

"What is it, Carole?" he asked absently, punching some numbers into the calculator and then making a note on a piece of paper.

"It's Ditto," she said. "He's still not working out. I've been trying and trying to get him to listen to me, but I haven't had any luck at all. We just aren't suited to each other. I'd like to try a different horse for the rest of the time before my horse gets here."

Barry looked up. "What was that?"

Carole repeated her request.

"I see," Barry said. "I'm sorry, Carole, but I'm afraid you're stuck with Ditto. We don't have any extra horses to put you on. Every available horse in the entire camp is already in use. Ditto was actually our spare—that's why you ended up on him when you decided not to bring your horse along. If you still want to switch after the second week, we'll have some free mounts when some of the campers leave." He glanced down at his calculator again and hit another button.

Carole frowned. "I won't need one then," she reminded Barry. "My horse is coming next Saturday, remember?"

"Oh, yes," Barry said, still looking at the calculator. Carole could tell he wasn't really listening to her.

She sighed with frustration. "Well, thanks anyway," she said. It came out sounding a little more sarcastic than she had intended.

But Barry didn't seem to notice. "Mmm hmm," he said. He appeared to be counting the feed bags stacked in the shed. "Anytime."

Carole left him and wandered across the field toward the mess hall. She was a little early for lunch, but she figured she could just sit and wait. If anything would make her feel better, it was a pep talk from her friends.

Stevie found her at their usual table twenty minutes later. "Hi," she said. "Any luck with Barry?"

"No," Carole replied with a sigh. "I'll tell you the whole story as soon as Lisa gets here."

"She's not coming," Stevie said.

Carole looked surprised. "Don't tell me she's too engrossed in *Lord of the Flies* to stop and eat?" That was the latest book Lisa was reading. She had brought it to breakfast with her and been so busy reading that she had hardly touched her eggs and toast.

"Not this time," Stevie said. "She and Piper are going to use the time to work on their dance routine for the talent show." The other day at dinner, Lisa and Piper had told them all about their plans. "She said something about a problem with the finale. I guess they're still ironing out the choreography."

Carole shook her head. "I don't know how they do it," she said, picking up her turkey sandwich. "Even after skipping trail class, I'm totally ravenous. No wonder Piper is so thin."

But Stevie was thinking about something else. "Speaking of the talent show," she said, "we've got to come up with an act soon." Stevie, Carole, and the other girls in their cabin had been discussing ideas all week. But so far nobody had come up with anything good, not even Stevie.

"I know," Carole said. "We only have a little over a week to rehearse as it is. Maybe we should have another cabin meeting tonight before lights-out."

"Good idea," Stevie said with a deep sigh. "I was hoping to invite Phil to go for a romantic stroll, but I haven't even seen him all day."

Carole nodded sympathetically. "Tonight it is, then. We'll find the others and tell them after we eat."

Stevie took a sip of her water. "Now that that's settled, tell me about your meeting with Barry."

MEANWHILE, IN CABIN SIX, Lisa was waiting for Piper to arrive for their rehearsal. While she waited, she reread part of the letter she had received that day. It was from her mother, and it was full of all sorts of chatty news and gossip about things that were happening at home and in Willow Creek. But it was the last paragraph that Lisa kept returning to:

> *You'll never guess who I met the other day, dear. Do you remember Mrs. Parrish, who used to baby-sit you when you were younger? Well, her daughter Susan just moved back to town. Susan's a licensed teen counselor, and I was telling her about your little problem with your report card. She thinks it might help if you came in and spoke with her when you get back from camp. What do you think about that? It's up to you, dear. But Susan Parrish is really very nice, and I think it might be good for you to . . .*

Lisa crumpled the letter angrily in her hand. She couldn't believe her mother was blabbing her personal problems all over town. If Lisa wanted everyone in Willow Creek to know about her bad grade, she would have taken out an ad in the paper. Besides, what did her mother think she could possibly have to talk about with a teen counselor, whatever that was? She hadn't studied hard enough, so she had gotten a low grade. End of discussion.

Just then Piper came in. "Ready to get started?" she asked.

Lisa tossed the crumpled letter into her cubby. "Ready when you are."

"Good," Piper said. "I was thinking about the finale during classes this morning, and I think I came up with something that might work. Can you do a split?"

"Hmmm?" Lisa said absently. She was still thinking about the letter. Was a counselor the same thing as a psychologist? Did her mother think she was crazy for getting such a low grade for no good reason?

"A split," Piper said. "Can you do one?" She paused, waiting for a reply. "Earth to Lisa!"

Lisa looked up, her face turning red. "Oh, sorry, Piper," she said quickly. "I—I guess I was thinking about something else." She hesitated, then added, "Actually, it was something my mother said in her last letter."

"What's the matter?" Piper asked, sitting down on the bunk next to her. "Anything you want to talk about?"

83

Lisa hesitated again. She did want to talk about it, but Piper was so perfect. Would she be able to understand Lisa's problems?

"Don't worry, I know how mothers can be sometimes," Piper added, rolling her eyes. "Mine can be a real pain."

"Really?" Lisa said, relieved. Without further ado, she poured out the whole story.

When she finished, Piper was nodding. "Your mother says you're nuts because you're upset about that grade. But I bet she's really more upset about it than you are," she said. "Believe me, I know exactly how you feel. My mom is just the same way. But I don't let it bother me anymore."

"But how?" Lisa asked. "I mean, she is my mother . . ."

"It doesn't matter," Piper said. "Mother, father, stranger, it *doesn't* matter. I can tell you're a lot like me, Lisa. When you do something, you like to do it right. But not everybody understands people like us."

Lisa nodded. She remembered her friends' reaction to her B+. "I know what you mean."

"You can't let other people's stupid opinions get in your way," Piper went on, taking Lisa's hand in her own and squeezing it. "Most of the time when they criticize you or laugh at you, it just means they're jealous. They don't understand why you're pushing yourself so hard, because they don't know how good it feels when you do something you've set out to do, and do it really well. If you let their comments bother you, that means they've won." She paused for a moment, and a sad look passed over her face. "It hasn't always been easy for me to remember that. But whenever I've given in to them, I've always been able to pull myself together again and try even harder."

Lisa was amazed. Piper seemed to know exactly how Lisa felt. She seemed to understand how important it was for Lisa to be the best—to strive for perfection in everything she did. But that made sense. After all, Piper herself was practically perfect. Lisa wondered what had made the other girl look so sad, but she didn't want to pry. Piper would tell her if she wanted to.

The two girls went outside and found a clear, even section of the path. As they did a few stretches and then started to try out parts of their dance number, Lisa couldn't help admiring the way Piper moved. The older girl's long, slender limbs moved with grace and power, never hesitating or failing. Lisa did her best to imitate her, and by the end of their rehearsal she was feeling pretty good. She wasn't as perfect as Piper yet, but after their talk she had new hope. All it took was hard work, and Lisa was good at that.

THE NEXT MORNING at breakfast, Stevie and Carole were still talking about the previous evening's cabin meeting.

"I can't believe Helen really wanted to put on a historical drama about the sinking of the *Titanic*," Stevie said, referring to one of their cabin mates.

"I know." Carole speared a sausage with her fork. "But at least that idea wasn't as ridiculous as Bev's. Who would have guessed she was a baton twirler?"

Lisa laughed. "You should have done what Piper and I did," she said. "Just decided what you wanted to do and told them."

"Maybe you two could come over and set our cabin mates straight," Carole said. "Where is Piper this morning, anyway?" The older girl sometimes sat with The Saddle Club for meals.

"She's working on figure eights with Tapestry," Lisa said. Thinking about Piper's dedication made her feel a little guilty. She set down her cereal spoon. She really should be working on her reading or her riding rather than wasting all this time sitting around chatting with her friends.

"The problem isn't *telling* our cabin what we want to do," Stevie reminded Carole. "It's *coming up* with something we want to do." She sighed. "And I can't think of a thing."

Before the discussion could go any further, Barry stood up and waved his arms for attention.

"I wonder if he has something exciting planned for today," Stevie whispered eagerly as the mess hall quieted down. "It is Saturday, you know." In previous years, Barry had always planned something special for the end of the first week of camp. One year it had been a trip to a local horse show; another time, a day trip to a nearby breeding farm. During The Saddle Club's first visit to Moose Hill, the big event had been an overnight trail ride.

"I hope so," Carole said. "I could use a break from

classes." *And from Ditto*, she thought, though she didn't say it.

Sure enough, Barry's announcement was about this year's first-Saturday-of-camp event. "This time we thought we'd do something a little different," he announced. "After lunch, I'd like everyone to gather in the meadow for a good old-fashioned picnic. There will be games and prizes, and for dinner we'll have a cookout over a roaring campfire, with all the hamburgers, hot dogs, and potato chips you can eat."

It all sounded like fun to The Saddle Club. Stevie raised her hand. "Will there be horseback games, or just regular people games?" she asked when Barry pointed to her.

Barry smiled. "Good question. We'll have games of both the two-footed and four-footed variety."

"Shouldn't that be six-footed?" Stevie called out.

Amid the laughter that greeted Stevie's remark, Carole overheard the girl sitting at the next table complaining to her friend.

"You'd think with all the money our parents are paying they could come up with something better than a stupid picnic," the girl said. "What a cheap treat." Her friend nodded.

Carole frowned. It was obvious that some people weren't in the proper camp spirit. But she wasn't going to let a couple of party poopers spoil *her* fun. There was nothing she loved more than horseback games. Then she remembered that she would be riding Ditto rather than Starlight. With that thought, her frown deepened.

AFTER MORNING CLASSES and a quick lunch in the mess hall, the campers gathered in the meadow. It was a perfect summer day, breezy and warm, with hardly a cloud in the sky.

Before starting the games, Barry announced that in addition to the small ribbons to be awarded for each game, there would be two grand prizes handed out at the end of the afternoon. One would go to the two-footed champion, the camper who had won the most ribbons in the non-riding games. The other, naturally, would go to the four-footed champion—though Stevie continued to insist that *six-footed champion* would be a more accurate term. Barry promised that if Stevie won, he would personally change the wording on the ribbon for her.

Then the fun began. The campers were kept busy running from game to game. First came the two-footed games: a sack race, a three-legged race, a water balloon toss, a wheelbarrow race, and others. Before long each member of The Saddle Club had several small, colorful ribbons pinned to her shirt.

The only thing that kept Stevie from enjoying herself

completely was Phil. At the beginning of the day she had assumed that this would be their chance to finally spend some quality time together. But somehow they never seemed to be in the same spot at the same time. And every time the counselors announced a pairs game, Phil and Todd ended up together, and Stevie was left to be partners with Carole or Lisa or one of the other girls in her cabin.

A whole week of camp had already passed, and none of Stevie's romantic plans had worked out. She knew that Phil was as busy as everybody else. And she knew that he wanted to make friends with the boys in his cabin. But still, she couldn't help thinking that he could have made a little bit of time to be with her if he really wanted to. That raised one big question in her mind: *Did he really want to spend time with her?*

About a dozen campers, including Carole and Phil, were lining up for the first heat of a somersault race when Stevie found Lisa sitting on the sidelines watching. She sat down beside her on the sun-warmed grass.

"Hi," Stevie said. "Having fun?"

Lisa pointed to the ribbons fluttering on her chest. "Three firsts, a second, and two thirds so far," she announced proudly. "At this rate I'll have the two-footed championship all sewn up."

"Don't count on it," Stevie said with a grin, glancing

down at her own T-shirt, which was crowded with almost as many ribbons as Lisa's. "I'm still in the running, you know."

Just then the starter's pistol fired, and the two girls watched as Carole and the others tumbled their way toward the finish line. Carole came in second. Phil, who had collided with another boy halfway through, was ninth.

"I'm in the next heat," Lisa said, standing up. "I'd better get up there. I want to get a starting position on the outside so there's less chance of anyone running into me and messing me up."

Stevie wished Lisa luck and then hurried over to congratulate Carole on her performance and tease Phil about his. When she reached the finish line, Carole was shaking her head, looking dizzy. Phil had already disappeared.

"Good race," Stevie told Carole. "Did you see where Phil went?"

"Sorry." Carole put a hand to her head. "I can't see much of anything right now."

"Never mind," Stevie said with a frown. "You don't have to be dizzy to miss him these days." She took Carole's arm and led her to a vacant spot on the sidelines to sit down.

"That's better," Carole said after a moment, when her

head had cleared. "Now what were you saying about Phil?"

"Oh, nothing," Stevie said with a sigh, watching as Lisa and the others in her heat lined up. "It's just the same old thing I've been saying all week. I've hardly seen him since we got to camp. So much for our month of romance."

"I thought I saw you talking to him after equitation class this morning," Carole said.

Stevie nodded. "I asked him if he wanted to sit together at the campfire tonight, and then walk down to the pond like we did the day we met." She sighed again. "I just hope he doesn't forget about it. I don't seem to be the first thing on his mind these days."

"He won't forget," Carole assured her. "This is Phil we're talking about, remember? He's crazy about you. I'm sure he's just been too busy this past week to show it. But I'll bet he makes up for it tonight." She winked. "A moonlit stroll down to the pond, a romantic kiss or two, and you'll forget you were ever worried about him." Her smile faded. "I just wish my problem was that easy to solve," she added.

"You mean Ditto?" Stevie asked, watching as the heat began and Lisa somersaulted her way into an early lead.

"What else?" Carole said. "I'm dreading the start of

the riding games. How can they possibly be any fun on a horse that's no fun to ride?"

Stevie hadn't thought of that. "That's too bad," she said. "You and Starlight are so good at mounted games."

"I know," Carole said. "It makes me miss him more than ever. Maybe I shouldn't even bother to play. Barry would probably let me just watch and cheer you guys on."

Stevie paused long enough to watch Lisa cross the finish line in first place. Then she turned to Carole. "Don't let Ditto totally ruin the day for you," she advised. "Even if he's not great at the games, it will still be more fun playing than watching."

Carole wasn't so sure that was true, but she agreed to give it a try.

TWO HOURS LATER, Carole was wishing Stevie had kept her advice to herself. She and Ditto had just finished dead last in an egg-and-spoon race, mostly because his trot was so choppy that she had had to hold him to a walk to avoid dropping the egg at every stride. It also hadn't helped that he had stood stock-still for a good ten seconds after the other horses had started, once again failing to respond to her command to move ahead.

She slid down off his back and handed her egg and spoon to a counselor. "That's it," she said as Stevie and Lisa walked toward her, leading Belle and Major. "I quit." The egg-and-spoon race was only the latest in a series of humiliations for Carole and Ditto. They had taken part in more than half a dozen mounted games, from an obstacle course to a blindfold race, and hadn't won a single ribbon.

Stevie looked at her in dismay. "You can't quit now," she protested. "We need you for the costume relay. It starts in a few minutes." The Saddle Club had planned to enter the relay race, in which riders had to dismount and change in and out of silly costumes, as a team, with Piper as their fourth member.

Just then Piper joined them, already mounted on Tapestry. The mare's shiny black coat gleamed in the sunlight. "Ready for the relay, girls?" Piper called.

"Not exactly," Stevie said. "I think we're having a mutiny." She pointed at Carole. "She doesn't want to be in the race with us."

"You don't want me in it," Carole assured Piper. "This horse is hopeless. If we're on your team, you're guaranteed to come in last."

Stevie tried to think of a way to change Carole's mind. She liked to win as much as anyone, but first place or last, she knew the race would be more fun if The

Saddle Club was together. Before she could come up with anything, Piper spoke up.

"We don't want to force you to play if you don't want to, Carole," she said. She turned to Lisa. "I bet that girl Melissa from Cabin One would ride with us. I don't think she's on a team yet."

Lisa nodded eagerly. "She'd be perfect. Her horse is super fast. With her on our team, we'd be unbeatable."

Before Stevie or Carole could say another word, the other two girls had ridden off to find Melissa and convince her to join their team. By the time Betty called the participants forward, it was all settled.

Carole watched from the sidelines as the teams lined up for the race. She was relieved not to be taking part, though she was a little surprised that her friends had let her off the hook so easily. Still, it was true that Ditto would have drastically reduced their chances. Who could blame them for wanting to do well? She told herself she would return Ditto to his stall after she watched the race. In the meantime she let him wander freely at the end of his lead, nibbling at the grass.

It was an exciting race, and the teams were neck and neck for the first three legs. But Melissa's horse was just as fast as Lisa had said, and she pulled ahead in the final leg to clinch first place for the team.

Lisa let out a cheer as Melissa sped across the finish

line. "We did it!" she cried. "Another blue ribbon! It's a good thing Carole didn't ride with us, or we never could have won."

Stevie looked at her, surprised. What Lisa said was true, but the way she said it wasn't very nice. Stevie was no stranger to competitive feelings, but she had learned the hard way that these silly games were more fun if you just relaxed and didn't take them too seriously. Right now Lisa seemed to be taking them very seriously indeed. Stevie wondered if she should say something to her friend.

As she was trying to think of the most tactful way to begin, she heard a loud, shrill whinny from a short distance away. She turned to see what was happening and immediately forgot all about Lisa. Carole was in the meadow nearby, desperately hanging on to Ditto's lead line as he snorted and danced and tossed his head, trying to get away. Stevie could tell that it was only a matter of time before he started bucking or rearing—and when he did, Carole could get hurt.

Stevie dropped Belle's reins, leaving her ground tied at the end of the racecourse. Then she hurried over to help. Luckily Ditto wasn't yet completely out of control, and with both Carole and Stevie there, he soon gave up and calmed down. A few minutes later he was nibbling at the grass as if nothing had happened.

"Thanks, Stevie," Carole said as soon as she had caught her breath.

"What happened?" Stevie asked.

"I was getting ready to take him inside when a grasshopper jumped right past his face," Carole said. "At first he didn't seem that scared, so I tried standing in front of him and speaking to him calmly and clearly. That always works with Starlight when he's starting to spook." She shrugged. "But it just seemed to get Ditto more upset. That's when he really started to freak out."

"Well, I think the whole thing may have upset you more than it upset him," Stevie commented, glancing at the horse. "He seems to have recovered completely."

Carole nodded. "I'm taking him inside," she said.

"You can't quit now!" Stevie exclaimed. "There are only a few more games to go. And the next one sounds really interesting." The next race was a new one to The Saddle Club. In it, the riders had to walk across the meadow on foot, followed by their horses. The trick was, they weren't allowed to use a lead rope or lead the horses by the mane. In fact, they weren't allowed to touch them at all. They had to convince them to follow using only their voices and body language. After a long day of games, Stevie suspected that most of the horses would be more interested in stopping for a grassy snack than following their riders. It should be a lot of fun.

"Right," Carole said. "If Starlight were here, it would definitely be interesting. But I can't even get Ditto to listen to me when I'm using all my aids. How am I possibly going to communicate with him when I can't even touch him?"

But Stevie wouldn't stop wheedling and pleading until Carole agreed to try one more game. At last she gave in.

"Fine," she said. "We'll try one more. But if we come in last again, this boy's going straight back to his stall." Stevie had to be satisfied with that.

A few minutes later two dozen campers and their horses lined up for the no-hands race. Carole didn't have much hope for a prize as she unclipped Ditto's lead line and stuck it in her pocket. She just hoped her horse didn't spook again and injure someone. But the Appaloosa looked perfectly calm as he stood among the other horses.

Carole took a few steps forward, then turned to face him. To her surprise, Ditto was watching her, his ears pricked forward. Barry wasn't using his starting gun for fear of spooking the horses. He stepped into the middle of the makeshift racecourse, lifted his hand, and let it drop.

And the race was on—though it was hard to tell at first. The riders immediately began calling to their horses, coaxing and cajoling them forward in every way they could think of. For a few seconds the animals didn't seem inclined to move. Several of them lowered their heads and began to graze, while a few snuffled at each other or gazed around lazily. The watching crowd laughed.

"Ditto," Carole called. "Come on, boy." She held out her hand and tried to make her voice as friendly as possible as she continued to call his name. To her surprise, Ditto took a step toward her, then another.

Carole backed up quickly. "That's it," she called to the horse. "This way, Ditto. That's a good boy."

She couldn't believe it, but Ditto was walking steadily now. Carole had to move quickly to stay ahead of him. By this time a few of the other horses were moving, too, including Belle and Tapestry. Most of the others, including Major, were still at the starting line. Phil's horse, Teddy, had actually taken a few steps backward and so was technically in last place.

Soon Carole and Ditto had enough of a lead to fight off all challengers. By the time they neared the end of the course, Carole had turned around and broken into a jog to stay ahead of Ditto, who was trotting. She kept an eye on him over her shoulder and continued to call him forward. A moment later they crossed the finish line.

"We won!" Carole exclaimed in disbelief as a couple of her cabin mates who hadn't taken part in the race came over to congratulate her. She was still muttering the same phrase over and over again when Piper and Tapestry crossed the finish line to take second place.

"Sure you won," Piper said, overhearing. She pulled Tapestry's lead line out of her pocket and clipped it on to the mare's halter. "You let your horse graze all during the last race. No wonder he wasn't in the mood for any more grass." She smiled, and Carole was pretty sure she was just kidding. But she didn't quite know what to say. Luckily, Betty came over just then with Carole's blue ribbon, and by the time Carole looked up from pinning it on her shirt, Piper was gone.

Stevie, who had come in third, joined Carole a moment later. "That was great!" she exclaimed, giving Carole a hug. "Aren't you glad I talked you into entering?"

"I sure am," Carole said, glancing up at Ditto. The Appaloosa was rolling his eyes at Belle, who was sniffing at him curiously. "I can't believe it. For some reason he decided to listen to me this time. This could be a real breakthrough in our relationship. If he keeps it up, I might even survive another week without Starlight."

"Does that mean you're going to play in the next game?" Stevie asked. "It's break and out." In break and out, the judge called out a gait, and the riders had two strides to get their horses into that gait. After a moment, the judge called out another gait. Again, riders had two strides to get their horses to make the change. Any horse that was too slow was eliminated, and the game continued until only one rider was left. The Saddle Club had played the game many times at Pine Hollow. "And I should warn you," Stevie added with a grin, "Belle and I are the undisputed champions at this game."

"Not for long," Carole joked back.

Her jovial mood didn't last long. When the game started, Ditto was back to his old tricks. He was eliminated in the very first round for cantering when he was supposed to trot.

Carole decided to give him one more chance and entered the next and final race, a forward-backward-forward walking race. As the name indicated, competitors simply had to ride at a walk through three laps of the course, convincing their horses to walk backward for the second lap. But Ditto didn't do any better in this race than he had in break and out. He refused to walk backward for a long moment. When Carole finally got him through the second lap, Ditto was far behind most of the others. Unbidden, he broke into a trot as if trying to catch up, and was eliminated.

"I guess I was wrong," Carole told Stevie and Lisa when they met in the tack room a few minutes later. "What Ditto and I had wasn't a breakthrough. It was just a fluke." The campers were all hurrying to put their horses away. As soon as they were finished, Barry was going to announce the grand prize winners. Then it would be time to gather around the campfire for dinner and a well-deserved rest.

Soon the campers were gathered in the meadow again, forming a large semicircle around Barry and Betty. Betty held the ribbons and trophies, preparing to hand them to Barry as he called the winners' names.

Barry announced the two-footed winners first. "In third place we have Lisa Atwood!" Lisa walked forward to receive her prize ribbon, but Stevie thought she didn't look very excited. Barry awarded second prize to a boy The Saddle Club didn't know. "And finally, the one you've all been waiting for," Barry said, holding up a large blue ribbon and a small plastic trophy, "our two-legged champion . . . Phil Marsten!" Phil grinned and did a little victory dance as he went forward to claim his prize.

Next came the four-legged winners. "There was a lot of close competition for this one," Barry said, glancing at the piece of paper he was holding. "Several names should be mentioned as runners up, including Todd Prather, Lisa Atwood, and our two-footed champ, Phil Marsten." The campers clapped politely. "But now for our prizewinners. Third place goes to Helen York. And Piper Sullivan was a close number two." He paused to hand out the yellow and red ribbons. "In first place, as our four—no, better make that our *six*-footed champion, is Stevie Lake, with a little help from the lovely Belle."

Stevie hurried forward. With a grin, she waited as Barry pulled a felt-tipped pen out of his shirt pocket and crossed off the word *four* on the ribbon, writing *six* in its place. "Are you happy now?" he asked with a smile as he handed it over along with the trophy.

"Very," Stevie replied.

"This is great," Carole said to Lisa as they watched Stevie head back toward them. "You both won something."

Lisa shrugged. "Stevie *won*," she said, her voice so low that Carole could hardly hear her over the noise of the other campers. "I just came in third."

Stevie had just reached her friends. "See?" she said, waving her blue ribbon. "Phil and I are both champions. This is just another sign that he and I are meant for each other." She waved at him across the clearing, and he waved back with a grin. "Maybe he'll finally remember that at the campfire."

The tired and hungry campers walked down the length of the field and gathered around the campfire that a couple of the counselors had started at the far end. Stevie looked around for Phil, sure that he would be saving her a seat. But when she spotted him, she saw to her dismay that he was sitting on the ground surrounded by Todd and a whole crowd of other boys, talking and laughing.

She walked over to him. Maybe he was expecting her to find them good seats. "Hi, Phil," she said.

He looked up and smiled at her. "Oh, hi, Stevie," he said. "Congratulations on your trophy."

"You, too," she replied. She waited, but Phil didn't say anything else. He went back to talking to Todd about a skateboarding competition he had seen on TV.

Could it be? Had he really forgotten their date? Stevie decided to try one more time. "Hey, Phil," she interrupted. "It looks like some of the burgers are almost ready. How about it?"

He glanced up again. "Huh? Oh, that's okay, you go ahead," he said. "I'll get one in a few minutes."

That was that. He had forgotten their plans again. As Stevie spun on her heel and stomped away to find her friends, she vowed that this would be the last time Phil would have the chance to forget. If he didn't want to spend time with her, that was fine. She didn't want to spend time with him, either—ever again.

As Stevie entered the mess hall the following evening, she saw Phil waving at her from his usual table. He gestured at the empty seat next to him, but Stevie turned away as if she hadn't seen. She was determined to stick to her vow.

"Come on," she said to Carole and Lisa. "I think I see a table over there." She pointed to the farthest corner of the hall.

When the girls were seated, Carole glanced across the room at Phil and saw that he was looking in their direction, a puzzled look on his face. She felt a little sorry for him. "Are you sure you shouldn't give Phil one more chance?" she asked Stevie.

"Are you kidding?" Stevie said, sprinkling salt on her food. "I gave him more than enough chances already. He used up the last one when he forgot about our plans last night."

"Maybe it was a mistake," Carole protested. "It was a pretty exciting day, and—"

"If that's true, then he's been making mistakes all week," Stevie interrupted.

She was looking annoyed, so Carole let the subject drop. The last thing she wanted was to get Stevie started about Phil. It was all she had talked about at the campfire the night before.

Carole picked up her fork. "You know, after yesterday I really had hopes for Ditto," she said, returning to the subject that had occupied most of her own thoughts lately. "But he was worse than ever today. Having that breakthrough—or what I thought was a breakthrough—makes it even harder to deal with him somehow."

"At least you only have five more days until Starlight gets here," Stevie pointed out.

Carole groaned. "Ugh, five whole days. I don't want to think about it. Let's change the subject." She turned to Lisa. "How's your reading going?"

Lisa shrugged. "Not as well as I'd like," she said, stifling a yawn. She had been staying up late every night, doing her best to work her way through her bag of books. "I started *Huckleberry Finn* last night, but I've only read a few chapters so far."

"Wow," Stevie said. "I can't believe you've read so many of those books already. I haven't even finished the magazine I brought with me."

"I really haven't read that many. I still have a lot to do." As Lisa thought about all the work still ahead of her, she felt a familiar knot of anxiety form in her stomach. She poked listlessly at her half-eaten dinner, which suddenly looked less appetizing. "Actually, I think I'll go try to read a few more chapters now before I meet Piper and the other girls for our dance rehearsal."

Carole glanced at Lisa's plate. "But you've barely touched your food," she said. "At least stay and finish eating."

"I'm full," Lisa said. "I had a big lunch." She stood up and hurried away before Carole or Stevie could protest any further.

Stevie shook her head as she watched Lisa depart. "I don't know how she does it," she said. "With everything else going on at camp, I can't even imagine worrying about doing schoolwork." She sighed. "Speaking of things that should be going on, we really have to figure out what to do for the talent show."

"I know," Carole said. "If we don't come up with something soon, we might as well forget about entering." She paused to take a sip of water. "The problem is, what can we do that everyone in the cabin will agree to?"

"We'll just have to talk some sense into Helen and Bev and the others," Stevie said firmly. "Why don't we have another cabin meeting tonight? We'll just make them all sit there until we can agree on something. Even if it turns out to be baton twirling."

Carole shook her head. "That's a good idea, but we can't do it tonight," she said. "We promised to help mix grain after dinner, remember?"

"I forgot," Stevie admitted. She frowned. "Why did Barry have to pick this year to start turning into Max?" Just as Betty had said on the first day, campers were expected to help out this year, and The Saddle Club had volunteered to mix the grain rations for the coming week.

"I guess Lisa forgot, too," Carole said.

"We can swing by her cabin and pick her up on our way to the grain shed," Stevie said.

Carole paused, remembering how tired Lisa had looked. "Maybe we shouldn't," she said. "She seems awfully worried about her reading. Maybe if we let her be she'll catch up a little and feel better. We can mix the grain without her."

108

"Okay," Stevie said. "Besides, that way we can talk about the talent show without boring her to death."

The girls continued to discuss ideas for the show as they finished eating. Then they got up and headed out of the mess hall. As they passed Phil's table, he called out their names. Carole automatically paused, but Stevie grabbed her by the elbow and dragged her forward.

"Don't say a word," she hissed through clenched teeth.

Carole obeyed, but Phil got up and hurried after them. "Hey, Stevie," he called. "Todd and I were talking about playing some tennis after dinner. How about it—are you and Carole up for another game of doubles?"

But Stevie continued toward the door without answering, and a moment later she and Carole were outside in the warm summer night. Phil didn't follow them. "Come on, let's cut through the stable on our way to the grain shed," Stevie said. "I want to stop in and say hi to Belle."

Carole agreed, figuring that after the encounter with Phil, Stevie could use a calming influence. The two girls hurried through the quiet stable to Belle's stall.

"Hey there, girlfriend," Stevie greeted her horse with a smile. She pulled out a couple of carrot pieces she had saved from her salad at dinner. "Here's a little something I had the chef whip up especially for you." She held the carrot pieces out and let the mare nibble them from her hand one by one.

As Carole watched Stevie with her horse, she felt a pang of homesickness—or, to be more accurate, horse-sickness. She missed Starlight more than ever. She wanted to be able to ride without worrying about whether her horse was going to understand her next command. Suddenly she didn't care whether she and Ditto had made a breakthrough during the no-hands race on Saturday or not. All she cared about was Starlight's arrival on the following Saturday.

A few minutes later the girls were in the grain shed, hard at work measuring and mixing feed. Betty had been there to show them what to do, but she had left to do some other chores.

As they worked, the girls tossed more talent show ideas back and forth. Nothing seemed quite right, and half an hour later they still hadn't come up with anything that they thought everyone in their cabin would like. In fact, they hadn't even come up with anything *they* liked.

Deciding it was time to give their brains a rest, Carole told Stevie what she had been thinking about back in the stable. "I just don't want to waste any more time figuring out what's wrong with Ditto," she said. "I only hope I can survive for five more days until Starlight gets here. Riding Ditto is so exhausting. I never know what he's going to do next."

Stevie had finished her part of their task and was resting on a pile of empty bags. Suddenly she sat bolt upright. "That's it!" she exclaimed.

"What?" Carole asked, looking up from the bag of rolled oats she was weighing.

"You just gave me a great idea," Stevie said. "I know the perfect kind of skit we can do for the talent show!"

Carole looked confused. "You do? What did I say?"

"It was what you just said about never knowing what's coming next from Ditto," Stevie explained. "Come on, hurry up and finish those oats and we'll be done here. I'll tell you about it on the way back to the cabin. It's time to hold that meeting!"

TWO DAYS LATER Stevie, Carole, and their cabin mates finished the first rehearsal of their new play. It had a simple title, *Cabin Three: The Play*, but the story was anything but simple. That was because it had been written by the entire cabin. Stevie's idea had been to pass a notebook around the cabin, with each girl contributing three lines at a time. That meant, for instance, that when Carole began the play by casting herself as a princess, Helen could—and did—add a plot twist wherein the princess just happened to be booked into a luxurious suite on the *Titanic*. And when Stevie took over, she cast herself as a powerful witch who rescued the princess from drowning in the icy sea when the ship went down and bestowed on her the gift of magical powers.

"That was great, guys," Stevie cried as soon as Bev, who played a baton-twirling congresswoman, had given her final speech.

"I don't know," Carole said. "I still think we need a better way to end it. An appeal for boating safety doesn't seem that exciting somehow."

Helen, who had written most of the final speech, pretended to pout. "Oh, come on," she protested. "It's thematic, isn't it?"

"I think Carole's right," Stevie said. She rubbed her chin thoughtfully. "We should have something more dramatic. I'll try to come up with something to tie up all the loose ends."

Carole wasn't sure that was possible, since more ends were loose than otherwise, but she nodded. "Great," she said. "Now let's go eat. All that great acting made me hungry."

Carole and Stevie said good-bye to their other cabin mates and walked to Cabin Six to pick up Lisa. "I really think this play is going to be terrific," Carole said. "It's so silly, it's sure to make everyone laugh—Barry included, even though he's been such a grump lately. It may have taken you longer than usual, but you definitely hit on a great idea this time, Stevie."

"Thanks," Stevie said. "But like I said, it was your comment about never knowing what Ditto would do next that made me think of it."

"I'm glad he served some purpose," Carole said, rolling her eyes.

The two girls had reached Cabin Six. They knocked, but there was no answer. Stevie opened the door and peeked inside.

"Lisa? Are you in there?" she called. "It's time for dinner."

There was no answer. "Maybe she went for a swim," Carole suggested. The two girls headed down the path through the trees toward the pond. Soon they could hear voices. When the pond came into view, they saw several campers splashing around in the shallows. They also saw Lisa, who was swimming laps across the deeper section of the pond.

Carole frowned. "What's she doing? It's not like she needs any more exercise after a hard day of riding." It didn't make sense. Suddenly Carole realized that a lot of things Lisa had been doing since arriving at camp didn't make a whole lot of sense—or at least they weren't much like Lisa's usual behavior. Carole glanced at Stevie. "Do you—do you think Lisa's all right? I don't think I've seen her relax since we got to camp."

Stevie shrugged. "Lisa has always been kind of intense." But Carole's words made her think. Maybe Lisa *had* been even more serious and hardworking than usual lately, especially considering that camp was supposed to be fun. Maybe she was pushing herself a little too hard. Stevie glanced over and saw her own worry reflected in Carole's brown eyes.

The two girls walked over to the edge of the pond. Just then Lisa raised her head to take a breath and spotted them. She waved and swam over to the beach.

"Hi," she said breathlessly, wiping water from her face. "Is your rehearsal over already?"

Carole nodded. "It went pretty well. I think the play will be a big hit at the talent show." She hesitated. She couldn't help wondering if she and Stevie should say something about how hard Lisa was pushing herself. If she couldn't even relax enough to enjoy a pre-dinner swim without turning it into a workout, maybe there was something wrong. "Um, why were you swimming laps just now?" she asked, trying to sound casual.

Lisa laughed and rubbed the back of her neck. "Don't make fun of me, okay?" she said. "My neck was stiff from reading in the same position for too long. I thought doing a few laps might stretch out the muscles. So far it seems to be helping a little."

Carole almost laughed with relief. Obviously, her worry had been ridiculous. Lisa was fine. "Oh. Okay. Good. I—we were just kind of worried. You've been working so hard, what with your reading list and all."

Stevie nodded. "You know what they say about all work and no play, right?"

Lisa laughed again. "Don't worry," she said. "I remember how to play. And to prove it, I have an idea. How about hitting the arts and crafts room after dinner? I've been dying to try the calligraphy set they have there."

Stevie and Carole traded relieved glances. This was the Lisa they knew and loved. "You're on," they said in one voice.

"Speaking of dinner, we're going to be late if we don't hurry," Carole said. "Hurry up and get changed—we'll wait for you."

"You don't have to do that," Lisa said. "Just save me a seat, and I'll meet you there." She rubbed her neck again. "A few more minutes of swimming and I'll be as good as new."

CAROLE AND STEVIE were almost finished with their spaghetti and meatballs by the time Lisa arrived, looking fresh and clean in shorts and a white T-shirt. "Sorry it took me so long," she said. "The hot water in the shower just felt so good. I couldn't resist staying in for a few extra minutes."

"That's okay," Stevie said. "We'll wait for you to eat."

"Don't worry about it." Lisa grabbed a roll and a handful of carrot sticks from the platter in the center of the table. "I'll just eat this stuff as we walk. If we don't get there early, someone else will grab the calligraphy set."

The girls were the first ones in the arts and crafts

room. Lisa took out the calligraphy set and sat down at one of the small, round tables in the room. Stevie picked up some colorful leather strips to weave herself a bracelet, and Carole decided to try watercolor painting.

"This really feels like camp, doesn't it?" Stevie commented after the girls had been working in silence for a few minutes. "This arts and crafts stuff, I mean. I'm glad they added it."

"Yeah," Lisa said. "Listen, have either of you ever read *Of Mice and Men?*"

"No," Stevie said, and Carole shook her head.

"Is that the next book on your list?" Carole asked.

"It's the one I'm reading now," Lisa said. She bent closer to the paper in front of her to examine the letters she had just inscribed with the calligraphy pen. The last one was a little smudged. She crossed out the line and started again. "I finished *Huck Finn* last night."

"I *have* read that one," Stevie said. "It's one of my favorite books. I love the part when Huck dresses up like a girl. Did you like it?"

Lisa shrugged. "Sure, I guess so," she said. "But anyway, I was just thinking it would be better if I knew what was going to happen in these books before I read them. It would help me read faster. All I have to do is find someone who's already read *Of Mice and Men* and get them to tell me about it."

Carole looked up from her painting. She was doing a portrait of Starlight standing in the back paddock at Pine Hollow. "But that's no fun," she said. "Why even bother reading if you already know the whole story before you start?"

"I don't have time to read for fun, Carole," Lisa said, crossing out another row of fancy, swirled letters. "I've got too much to do. Piper and I have a ton of stuff to work on before Friday if our dance is going to be any good. We've still got a couple of rough spots in the choreography, and we promised to help the others practice their jumps. Some of them still can't do the harder moves right, and they're having trouble keeping up with the pace of the music. Plus Piper and I are dancing the lead in the big finale, and I haven't quite gotten the steps down yet. Besides all that, we've hardly even started talking about costumes." She dropped her pen on the table. "I don't know how we're going to get it all done in time."

Lisa was starting to look so anxious that Carole decided to change the subject. "Speaking of time, I don't know how I'm going to stand the rest of my time with Ditto," she said. "I know all I have to do is wait it out, but he's driving me crazy. Any advice?"

Stevie opened her mouth to answer, but Lisa stood up. She didn't seem to have even heard Carole's question.

"Listen, this has been fun, but I'd better get going," she said. She hurriedly scooped up the calligraphy set and returned it to its place. Then she dumped the paper she had been practicing on in the trash can and headed for the door. "I want to find Piper and talk to her about those costumes. See you later."

"Bye," Stevie said. When Lisa had gone, she glanced at Carole. "Looks like it's just the two of us again."

Carole nodded. "That's starting to be an awfully familiar feeling." She sighed. "Suddenly I'm not in the mood for painting anymore."

"I know what you mean," Stevie said. She stuck her half-finished bracelet in her pocket. "Come on, let's go."

A FEW MINUTES later Carole and Stevie were lounging on their bunks. Their cabin mates had all gone swimming, so they had the place to themselves.

"Do you think we should say something to Lisa about the way she's acting?" Carole asked. Her earlier worries about her friend were starting to return.

"You mean, like Superwoman?" Stevie said. She shrugged. "I don't know. You know how she is when she sets her mind to something. The trouble is, this time she's set her mind to *everything*."

"I know," Carole said. "I'm starting to get really worried about her. She didn't even seem to remember we were in the room just now, not even when I asked for help with Ditto."

"By the way, I never got a chance to give you my advice about that," Stevie said. "I think you should just grit your teeth and do your best to pretend you're already riding Starlight."

"Easier said than done," Carole said. "Ditto and Starlight are practically polar opposites. Starlight is so wonderful, and Ditto—well, I know Max would probably say I'm crazy, but sometimes I think Ditto goes out of his way to be obnoxious and stubborn." She rolled her eyes. "In fact, he probably followed me in that no-hands race just to throw me off track."

"Wait," Stevie said. "That's it!" She jumped up from the bunk and waved her hands excitedly. "You've done it again, Carole. You've just given me an idea for the perfect ending to our play!"

"What's—" Before Carole could finish her question, the cabin door swung open with a bang. Lisa stood in the doorway, wild-eyed and breathless.

"Piper," she gasped. "She's gone!"

IT TOOK CAROLE and Stevie a few minutes to calm Lisa down. "Now, what's this about Piper?" Stevie asked. "What do you mean, she's gone?"

"I went back to the cabin to talk to her about our

120

dance costumes, like I said," Lisa explained. She was sitting on the edge of Carole's bunk, her arms wrapped around her body as if she were cold. "I didn't see her there, so I went to the stable. She wasn't there, either, and Tapestry was in her stall. I checked the rec hall, the pond, everywhere I could think of, and nobody I asked had seen her. I figured she must have gone for a run or something, so I went back to the cabin to read and wait for her, and that's when I noticed her stuff was gone."

"Gone?" Stevie repeated. "Why would she leave right in the middle of camp without telling anyone?"

"I don't know." Lisa's face was pale and worried. "Maybe she ran away. Maybe she was kidnapped! I think her parents have a lot of money—maybe she's being held for ransom!"

"Hold on a minute," Carole said, holding up one hand. Normally Lisa was the sensible one of the three, but it seemed that someone else was going to have to step in this time and think logically. "What kind of kidnapper would pack up someone's suitcase and take it along? Anyway, someone would notice if a stranger drove up and grabbed a camper in broad daylight."

"It's dark out now," Lisa pointed out. "Besides, we've seen strange cars around all week. Remember that black gangster-type car that was parked along the driveway?" But she seemed to realize that the kidnapping theory was pretty unlikely. "Anyway, even if she just ran away, she's all alone. If she's wandering around in the woods somewhere, she could get hurt."

"Why would she run away?" Stevie asked.

But Carole was already shaking her head. "I don't know Piper as well as you do, Lisa," she said, "but I do know one thing about her. She's crazy about her horse. If Tap is still in the stable, I can guarantee that Piper didn't run away. She must have had to leave suddenly for some kind of emergency."

"But why?" Lisa asked. "Why would she have to leave? She didn't say anything to me about it when I saw her after class this afternoon."

Carole was trying to remember the last time she'd seen Piper. "Come to think of it, I don't think she was at dinner," she said.

Lisa shrugged. "That's no big deal," she said. "I just assumed she was jogging or riding or something." She looked up at her friends. "So what should we do?"

"I guess we could go ask Barry about it," Stevie said. "If Piper had to rush away for a family emergency or something, I'm sure he'd tell us."

Carole offered Lisa a candy bar, but Lisa waved it away. "Not now," she said. "I just want to find Piper. Let's go talk to Barry."

The girls hurried to Barry's office, but he wasn't there. "He had to go into town. He won't be back until late. Is there anything I can help you with?" asked his assistant, a young man with a limp brown ponytail.

"We wanted to ask him about my cabin mate, Piper," Lisa said. "Piper Sullivan. She seems to have disappeared, and I'm worried about her."

The assistant's pleasant smile turned to a frown. "Oh, her," he said. "She's gone. And don't bother to ask why, because Barry wouldn't tell me." He shrugged. "All I know is, she's not coming back."

"Is she sick?" Lisa cried. "Is she hurt? You have to tell me!"

The assistant shrugged again. "I told you, I don't know," he said. "Barry just said something about personal reasons. If you want to know any more, you'll have to take it up with him tomorrow."

"Don't worry," Lisa said, as Carole and Stevie led her away. "I will."

THE NEXT DAY in equitation class, Carole and Stevie had a chance to talk while the instructor was working with another student.

"Hey, Carole," Stevie said. "You still haven't given me a yes or no on my idea for the ending of our play."

"Yes I did," Carole replied, rolling her eyes. "I already said no. You just refuse to accept it." After returning from Barry's office the evening before, Stevie had finally had a chance to tell Carole and the other girls in their cabin about her idea.

"Oh, come on. The others loved the idea," Stevie said. She gave Carole her most charming smile. "Just say you'll do it. Please? Pretty please with sugar on top?"

Finally Carole laughed and gave in. "All right, I'll try," she said. "For the sake of the play. But don't blame me if—"

"Hi," Phil said, riding up and interrupting Carole's comment. "What's up?"

Stevie moved Belle a few steps away. "Anyway, Carole," she said, her voice icy. "I don't think we should rehearse the ending. It will be better if we just let it happen sort of spontaneously, you know?"

Carole glanced from Stevie to Phil and back again. She sighed. "All right," she said weakly. She hated being caught in the middle of Stevie and Phil's fight—even though she wondered if Phil had even realized that they were fighting. "No rehearsing."

Just then the instructor clapped his hands for attention. "Okay. We have time for one more exercise," he called out. "Everyone find a partner."

Phil pulled Teddy up beside Belle. "How about it, Stevie?" he said with a smile. "Will you be my partner?"

Stevie didn't reply. She just turned to Carole. "Let's be partners, Carole," she said. "Come on, let's move to the other side of the ring. It's getting a little crowded over here." She rode off. With an apologetic glance at Phil, Carole followed.

AFTER CLASS, STEVIE and Carole found Lisa waiting for them outside the stable. As the three girls walked toward the mess hall for lunch, Lisa gave the others the latest update on Piper's disappearance.

"I'm sure you've noticed that Tapestry is gone now, too," Lisa said.

Carole nodded. She had passed the tall black mare's stall several times that morning. It was empty and swept clean. "I guess that means Piper really isn't coming back."

"There are all sorts of rumors around camp about what happened," Lisa said. "A lot of people are saying that someone in Piper's family died. Others think she got food poisoning from the mess hall. Some heard she was suddenly hired as a fashion model and had to rush off to Paris for a shoot. One person even seemed to think that Piper had stolen Tapestry from a major racing stable and was arrested." She rolled her eyes. "And a few people—including Phil's friend Todd—are sure she was abducted by aliens."

"I think we can safely rule out that last one," Carole said with a laugh.

"And the one about the food," Stevie added. "We've all been eating it, and nobody else got sick. Besides, Piper didn't even go to dinner the day she disappeared—or most other days, for that matter."

"Anyway, I tried to call her house this morning from the phone in the rec hall," Lisa said. "There was no answer. I also tried to talk to Barry about it, but he just said the same thing his assistant told us—that Piper had to leave for personal reasons. Then he claimed to have some important phone call to make and shut himself in his office." She sighed. "This is terrible. I'm not going to be able to stop worrying until I find out what happened to her."

"At least you'll get to move in with us in a few days," Carole said. One of the girls in Cabin Three was leaving on Saturday, and Carole and Stevie were sure that Barry would let Lisa take her place in their cabin. "Maybe then you won't miss her so much."

By this time the girls had arrived at the mess hall. "Come on," Stevie told Lisa. "Let's go in. We can talk more about this at lunch."

126

"Lunch? Are you kidding?" Lisa said. "I don't have time. Now that Piper's gone, I have more to do than ever. For one thing, I want to go try to call her again. Plus it looks like I'm on my own for the talent show. It's in two days, you know. I've got to figure out what to do about costumes, and try to fix the choreography, and arrange the next rehearsal. . . . Besides, I was so distracted by everything last night that I didn't even pick up *Of Mice and Men*. I've got to make up for it today."

"But you've got to eat," Carole said. "You can do some of that stuff after lunch. You'll have a little time before afternoon classes start. Maybe we can help you."

Lisa shook her head. "Thanks, but that won't work," she said. "I need to use the time before classes to put in a little extra work with Major. If he's going to be a contender in that show-jumping event, he's got to be quicker at lengthening his stride after a turn." Before her friends could protest further, she hurried away toward her cabin.

Carole and Stevie went into the mess hall. As they sat down at their usual table, Carole let out a heavy sigh.

"Are you worried about Lisa?" Stevie asked.

"Well, yes, a little," Carole said. "I think this Piper thing is really bothering her a lot. And she doesn't seem to want to let us help her through it. But that wasn't what I was just thinking about. I was thinking about what she said about working on lengthening Major's stride. I've practically forgotten what it's like to have a horse I can work with like that. With Ditto, I'm lucky if he'll even give me the stride I ask for, let alone lengthening or shortening it."

"I thought you decided not to think about him anymore," Stevie said as she helped herself to some applesauce. "Starlight will be here in three days, and then you'll be home free."

"I know." Carole paused and frowned a little. "I guess it's still bugging me, though. Before I got Starlight I used to ride all sorts of horses—difficult ones, stubborn ones, even poorly trained ones—and I never had this much trouble."

"There's a first time for everything," Stevie said.

"I know," Carole said again. She let out another long sigh. "But this isn't what riding camp was supposed to be like."

FRIDAY, ANOTHER PERFECT summer day, was the day of the talent show. Afternoon classes were cut short in honor of the occasion, so right after an early dinner all the campers scurried back to their cabins to put on their costumes and make other last-minute preparations. Soon campers and staff were gathered in the meadow in front of the makeshift stage—actually just a patch of the meadow that had been mowed extra close to the ground. Several of the counselors had dragged hay bales out to serve as seating for the audience. Everyone sat down and waited. The only one missing was Barry, who was supposed to act as emcee for the show.

"Just hang in there, kids," Betty called, stepping to the front of the stage. "I'm sure he'll be here soon."

But five minutes passed, and Barry still hadn't arrived. "I'll go look for him," offered his assistant. He ran off toward the rec hall, his ponytail flopping behind him.

Stevie was sitting cross-legged on a bale with Carole and Lisa, trying not to look at Phil, who was nearby, trying to catch her eye. "Carole, is everything ready to go? I mean, your special prop?"

Carole nodded, nearly dislodging her tall, conical princess hat, which she and Stevie had made the evening before in the arts and crafts room. "Ready and waiting, just like the rest of us."

Ten minutes later, just as Betty was about to give in and take over as emcee, Barry's assistant reappeared. "He's on his way," the young man announced. Sure enough, Barry himself arrived soon after that.

"Sorry I'm late," he said. "I, uh, got caught up in something at the office." He smiled, though Lisa thought it looked a little forced. She wondered if his tardiness had something to do with Piper. She still hadn't managed to find out anything about her cabin mate's disappearance. Barry refused to tell her a thing, and every time Lisa tried to call Piper's house, the line was busy or there was no answer.

But Barry didn't give any further explanation. "Okay, let's get started," he said. "For the very first act of the first annual Moose Hill talent show, let's have a warm welcome for the talented girls of Cabin Two!"

With that, the talent show began. After Cabin Two, Barry called Phil's cabin to the stage. Unlike many of the other performers, the boys were wearing ordinary clothes.

"Do you know what they're doing for their act?" Carole asked. Then she remembered that Stevie was still mad at Phil. "Oh, sorry. Never mind."

"I can guess what they're doing," Stevie said. She frowned and crossed her arms across her chest. "It probably has something to do with skateboarding."

But she was wrong. There wasn't a skateboard in sight as the boys began their act. Phil stepped to the front of the stage. After tipping an imaginary hat, he announced, "The gentlemen of Cabin Eight proudly present, for your viewing pleasure, a vaudeville extravaganza. You'll laugh, you'll cry, you'll throw money—at least we hope so." He stepped back, and two of the other boys came forward. One was carrying a small wooden flute, which he began to play as the other boy did a silly dance.

Stevie was surprised. She would never have guessed it, but the boys really did seem to be trying to re-create an old-fashioned vaudeville variety show. It was exactly the kind of idea she might have come up with herself.

The flute player continued to play quietly in the background as the other boy stopped dancing and stepped forward. "This camp is great," he said to the audience. "There's so much to do. For instance, just yesterday I spent the whole evening playing backgammon with my horse."

The boy with the flute stopped playing and pretended to be amazed. "Really? Your horse can play backgammon? He must be really smart!"

The other boy shrugged. "Not really," he replied. "I won almost every game." He grinned while the audience groaned, then went on. "By the way, that reminds me of a riddle. What did the pony say when he got a sore throat?"

"What?" called out several campers from the audience.

"Nothing," the boy replied. "He was a little hoarse."

Everyone laughed at that one, including Stevie. Even though she was still mad at Phil, she had to admit that his cabin had come up with a great idea for the talent show. And she strongly suspected that Phil himself might have had something to do with that idea.

After telling a whole string of equally silly jokes and

riddles, the boy onstage held up his hands. "You've been very kind, ladies and gentlemen," he said. "Now for my final riddle. How did the raisin know he was being fired from his job?" The boy paused, then gave the answer. "He heard it through the grapevine." He raised one eyebrow. "And boy, was he surprised—he was expecting a grape raisin his salary!"

Stevie smiled as the rest of the audience groaned. She recognized that one—she had told it to Phil not long ago. She almost laughed out loud before remembering that she was mad at him. No matter how clever he was, he had been a jerk, and she wasn't going to forget it.

"Thank you, thank you!" the boy onstage cried as he and the flute player took their bows and the audience applauded enthusiastically. "I don't know what to say. We're so grapeful for your kindness!"

The audience laughed and clapped harder than ever, and the two boys took a final bow and backed away.

Then Phil and Todd came forward. "I heard there was a horse called Belle at this camp," Phil began.

Todd pretended to look surprised. "You can call a horse with a bell?" he asked. "I never heard of such a thing."

"No, no," Phil said. "You don't call this horse *with* a bell. You *call* her Belle."

"Why would you call a bell a horse?" Todd replied with an exaggerated shrug. By this time the audience was giggling. "That's just plain ridiculous."

"I'm not calling a bell a horse, you idiot." Phil pretended to smack the other boy. "I'm calling a horse a bell. I mean, I'm calling the horse Belle."

"Why call a horse a bell?" said Todd, scratching his head. "Why not just call a horse a horse?"

Phil let out a loud sigh and raised his hands to the heavens. "I can see I'm going to need a little help with this one." He shaded his eyes with one hand and peered out into the audience, pretending to search for someone. Finally he said, "Aha!" and pointed at Stevie. "I think I see just the young lady who can help me. Miss Stephanie Lake, will you come up here, please?"

Carole and Lisa glanced at Stevie, wondering what she would do. It was obvious that Phil was up to something, and it had nothing to do with Belle. Stevie sat still for a moment, and her friends were afraid she was going to ignore Phil's call.

Finally she stood up and walked forward. No matter how mad she was at Phil, she didn't have the heart to make him look stupid in front of the whole camp. But that didn't mean he was off the hook. She glared at him. "What do you want?"

He took her hand and pulled her onto the stage, turn-

134

ing her to face the audience. "I want you to help me clear something up," he said. "What's your horse's name?"

"Belle," Stevie said.

Todd poked her in the shoulder. "Didn't you hear him?" he demanded. "Now, stop talking about bells and tell us your horse's name, will you?"

"I just did," Stevie said. "Her name is Belle."

Todd put his hands on his hips. "Well, I certainly hope her name rings a bell," he said disapprovingly. "After all, she's your horse. Now what's her name?"

"Belle," Stevie said. "That's her name."

"Where?" Todd asked, pretending to look around.

By this time, Stevie was working hard to keep from smiling. She was having fun in spite of herself. "What's *his* name?" she asked Todd, pointing at Phil.

Todd looked a little confused, but he shrugged good-naturedly and answered, "Phil."

"That's right," Stevie said. "And I'm going to *fill* your shorts with grasshoppers if you don't shut up and listen. My horse's *name* is *Belle*."

"Oh!" Todd said. He shrugged and gave the audience a big grin. "Well, why didn't you say so in the first place?"

The performers, including Stevie, joined hands and took a bow. As the audience applauded, Phil squeezed

135

Stevie's hand a little tighter and leaned toward her. "We need to talk," he whispered. "I want to apologize for the way I acted before. Will you go for a walk with me after the show? Please?"

Stevie couldn't resist him when he was being so humble. She smiled and nodded, and Phil looked relieved.

"Let's have an extra round of applause for our lovely volunteer from the audience, Stevie Lake!" he announced, raising her arm over her head. The audience cheered loudly as Stevie returned to her seat.

"So, are you and Phil friends again?" Carole asked as Stevie sat down next to her.

Stevie smiled. "Almost," she said. "We're going for a walk after the show so he can apologize."

After a few more cabins performed, it was Lisa's turn. "Wish me luck," she muttered to her friends as she stood up, tugging at her costume. The five remaining residents of Cabin Six were wearing matching black T-shirts and denim cutoffs. "I'm going to need it."

"You'll do great," Stevie said, trying to reassure her. Lisa looked pale and nervous. "You always do."

Lisa and her cabin mates took the stage. One of them set a battery-operated cassette player in one corner of the stage and switched it on. A fast-paced jazz number poured out of the speaker, and the five girls began to dance. They started off with a staggered kickline, then moved straight into an intricate series of steps. The girls' feet moved so fast that it was hard for the audience to keep up.

Carole and Stevie couldn't take their eyes off Lisa as she danced. "Wow," Stevie whispered. "She's good!"

Carole nodded, gasping as all five girls leaped across the stage at once, perfectly in synch. "No wonder she spent so much time on this. It must have taken a lot of work to get everyone to do so well—especially since Lisa told us most of the girls in the cabin have never taken a single dance lesson."

All the girls danced well, but Lisa stood out from the rest. Her leaps and kicks were higher, her moves were smoother, and her arms arched more gracefully than theirs. At the end of the number, she did a few showy solo dance steps, cartwheeled to the front of the line, and then ended with a split, raising her arms high over her head as the other girls dropped to their knees behind her.

Carole and Stevie jumped to their feet and applauded wildly. Soon the whole audience followed their example. The girls from Cabin Six stood up and bowed, then ran off the stage and returned to their seats.

Lisa was breathing hard when she rejoined her friends.

"Lisa, you were fantastic!" Carole exclaimed, grabbing her friend and hugging her.

Stevie waited her turn, then gave Lisa a hug of her own. "You really were great," she added. Pulling back, she noticed that Lisa's eyes were brimming with tears. "Hey, what's wrong? You didn't hurt yourself, did you?"

Lisa shook her head. "I almost wish I did," she said, her voice sounding bitter and angry. "Then at least I'd have an excuse for all the mistakes I made."

"What mistakes?" Carole asked. "You looked perfect to me."

"I was off the beat during the second set of leaps," Lisa said, sitting down on the hay bale and wiping at her eyes. "And I took a big misstep right before my cartwheel at the end."

"Don't be so hard on yourself," Carole said comfortingly. "Nobody noticed those things. You were definitely the best one up there. The other girls weren't nearly as good as you."

"It doesn't matter how good they were," Lisa said. "It just matters how good *I* was. Or wasn't."

Before Carole and Stevie could think of anything to say to that, Barry called their cabin number. "Well, they say laughter is the best medicine," Stevie said to Carole as they hurried up to the stage. "And if anything can make Lisa laugh, it's our play."

As the premiere performance of *Cabin Three: The Play*

began, Carole and Stevie were too busy to notice if Lisa was laughing. But one thing was certain—even if she wasn't, everyone else was. The audience howled with laughter as Carole flitted onstage, trying her best to look like a dainty princess. They laughed even harder when Stevie intoned, "But the year was 1912, and tragedy was about to strike the fair princess. For her parents, the king and queen, had decided to send her on vacation— aboard the *Titanic*!"

The play continued to get sillier and sillier, as Stevie the Good Witch blessed Princess Carole with magical powers, which she went on to use to help Congresswoman Bev win the big election and save the world.

Finally, it was time for Carole to go and prepare for the big finale. She slipped away as Helen, who was playing a famous movie star, begged the congresswoman to tell them more about boating safety. By the time Bev's speech was finished, Carole was back, leading Ditto. She hadn't bothered with tack; she had simply slipped a halter on him. The horse seemed a little confused when she led him onto the stage, but he stayed calm.

"Why, hello, magical princess Carole," Stevie the Good Witch greeted her. "I see you've brought your horse."

"He's not a horse, you silly witch," Carole replied in

her princess's voice. "He's my pet unicorn, Ditto. I brought him to prove to you all that I truly am the royal princess of the land of Toodle-dee-doo."

"He doesn't look like a unicorn to me," Helen the movie star said.

"He most certainly is a unicorn," Carole replied haughtily. "He just happened to be born with a slight birth defect."

"What's that?" asked Helen.

Carole pointed to Ditto's forehead. "No horn. See?"

Congresswoman Bev crossed her arms over her chest and pretended to look suspicious. "Oh, really?" she said. "How do we know he's really a unicorn if he doesn't even have a horn?"

"I can prove it," Carole said. "Just watch, and I'll lead him with his invisible lead line." As she snapped off Ditto's lead line, Carole prayed that the laughter from the crowd wouldn't spook him. She stuck the lead in her pocket, then pantomimed pulling out an invisible one and clipping it on his halter. Then she took a few steps back and took a deep breath. This was the moment of truth.

She took a step backward, calling and gesturing and pretending to tug on the invisible lead. Ditto gave her a suspicious look, but finally he took a step in her direction. Carole continued to back away, and Ditto continued to follow, until they reached the far end of the stage.

Carole smiled with relief. Stevie's idea had worked. "Ta-da!" she cried, snapping the real lead line back onto Ditto's halter.

As the crowd erupted into applause and Ditto rolled his eyes nervously, Carole gazed at the horse. She had been skeptical about this whole plan. Ditto was so ornery, she was sure he would mess up the whole thing. Why hadn't he? Why would he pay attention to her in this one rather unusual way and not in any other? Carole didn't think even Starlight would follow her so obediently without any aids other than her voice.

Suddenly Carole realized what the answer might be. She gasped. "Oh, Ditto," she whispered under the noise of the crowd. "Could that be it?" Naturally, Ditto didn't reply. He just gave her his usual suspicious look.

Carole had to find out if her theory was correct. And she had to find out now. This might be her last chance before Starlight arrived in the morning. "Witch Stevie, give me a leg up," she called.

Stevie looked surprised, and Carole knew that this time she wasn't acting. "Are you sure?" she asked. "Er, I mean, surely your highness doesn't mean to ride without tack."

"I will ride without tack, because that is the only way that unicorns are ridden," Carole replied, making up the lines as she went along. "Now do my bidding, if you please."

Stevie stepped forward and hoisted Carole onto Ditto's back. He shifted uneasily under her, and she grabbed a handful of his mane to steady herself. She was going to have to do this without reins, which would make things more challenging. But suddenly she was sure she could do it.

"Out of the way, minions!" she cried to her fellow actors, waving her free arm above her head. "Now that everyone knows I am the true princess, I must ride off on my trusty unicorn to do good all over the world." With that, she signaled with her legs for a trot. But this time, she didn't signal lightly, as she would with the alert and sensitive Starlight. Instead she made the command as firm and unmistakable as she could.

And this time Ditto understood her. He broke into a trot almost immediately. When she signaled again, just as firmly, for a canter, he obeyed that command as well. They rode around the perimeter of the stage while the other actors took their bows, and Carole grinned as she heard the audience break into applause. Ditto broke stride for a moment at the noise, but even that didn't wipe the smile off his rider's face. Ditto wasn't perfect—

far from it—but Carole had finally realized that she was equally to blame for their poor relationship. She had come to camp wishing she could ride Starlight and ended up on a horse that was nothing like him. Then instead of adjusting to Ditto's unique personality, Carole had waited for the horse to adjust to her expectations, and that just wasn't going to happen.

She had figured it out just in time. She couldn't wait to share her discovery with Stevie and Lisa. Carole rode Ditto off the stage and toward the stable, silently promising him an extra ration of oats as a reward for his performance in the play. His gaits were still choppy and hard to ride, especially bareback, but for once Carole hardly noticed. She knew that the applause she still heard behind her was for their play, but she felt as though it was all for her. And she felt she deserved it, too.

THE NEXT MORNING after breakfast, The Saddle Club walked up to the hill by the stable to wait for Starlight to arrive.

"After he gets here, we'll help you move your stuff into our cabin," Carole promised Lisa. Their departing cabin mate had already been picked up by her parents, and Barry had approved the move.

"Thanks," Lisa said. She sat down on the grass and yawned.

"In the meantime," Stevie said, "I think this is the perfect time for a Saddle Club meeting." She turned to Carole. "I'm still waiting to hear what happened with

144

Ditto yesterday." The three girls hadn't had much time to talk since the talent show. After the show ended, Stevie had left immediately for a very long walk with Phil, and Lisa had rushed back to her cabin to read. There hadn't been much of an opportunity to talk at breakfast, either, since Lisa had come in late and Stevie had been busy talking with Phil.

"Good," Carole said. "I've been dying to tell you, even though I'm a little embarrassed at how stupid I was." She flopped down on the grass near Lisa, and Stevie sat down between them. Carole glanced quickly at the road when she heard the sound of an engine. But it wasn't coming from the Pine Hollow van; it came from a small blue car arriving to pick up a camper who was leaving. Carole went on. "I realized the reason I was having so much trouble with Ditto was that I was trying to turn him into Starlight."

Stevie looked puzzled. "What do you mean?"

"I mean I was doing everything the way Starlight likes it and not even noticing that it wasn't working," Carole explained. "For instance, Ditto is much more skittish and jumpy than Starlight, but I kept forgetting that. And Ditto hates being touched on the neck, but since I'm so used to patting Starlight there I kept doing it anyway, which must have made Ditto like me even less. Most importantly, when it comes to riding aids, Starlight

145

prefers a light touch, but Ditto needs a heavier hand. I should have realized that right away and changed what I was doing, but I was too busy missing Starlight." She shrugged. "If I'd been riding Basil, I probably could have gotten away with it. But Ditto is nothing like Starlight, so it just didn't work."

"I get it," Lisa said. "But I can't believe that you didn't figure it out for a whole two weeks. I mean, you've got so much riding experience . . ."

Carole shrugged. "It just goes to show, you're never done learning when it comes to riding," she said quietly. "And sometimes you even need to learn the same lessons over again, like this time. Once upon a time I would have figured Ditto out right away. Even if I wasn't crazy about him, I would have taken it as a challenge to bring out the best in him instead of the worst. A good rider can ride any horse well—and for a while there, I wasn't acting like a good rider."

"Well, Max will be glad you learned something," Stevie said. "Even if you had to spend two weeks riding a horse you didn't like to do it."

"I know," Carole said with a laugh. "Before, I was kind of mad at him for convincing me to do this. But now I'm almost glad. Although," she added hastily, "I might not be saying that if I didn't know Starlight was on his way here right now." She sighed, closing her eyes and enjoying the feel of the warm sun on her face. "He's the only thing missing to make camp perfect."

"Well, not the *only* thing," Lisa muttered.

Stevie turned over on her other side to look at her. "I hope you're not still thinking about those mistakes you claim to have made last night."

"Actually, I was thinking about Piper," Lisa said. "I'm beginning to wonder if I'll ever find out what happened to her." She paused as the blue car drove noisily past on its way out. "But now that you mention it, the dance thing is still bothering me a little. I shouldn't have made those mistakes."

Carole shrugged. "I really don't think you should beat yourself up about it, Lisa. You were practically perfect last night."

"Practically doesn't count," Lisa said, picking a blade of grass and rolling it between her fingers. "I wanted to be *totally* perfect."

"Nobody's *totally* perfect," Stevie said. "Except maybe Starlight, if you believe everything Carole says about him."

Carole smiled, but Lisa didn't even respond to the joke. "But I've got to try to be perfect," she said earnestly. "Or at least close to it, like Piper. If you can't strive for perfection, what's the point of doing anything?"

147

To Stevie, that seemed like an awfully philosophical question for a beautiful Saturday morning. But she could tell Lisa was serious. "I don't know," she said. "But I do know that you were a lot closer to perfect last night than I could have been."

"That goes double for me," Carole put in. "I've got two left feet when it comes to dancing. Dad says it runs in the family. I could hardly believe the way you made all those hard moves look so easy, Lisa."

"Besides," Stevie said, "as far as most of this camp knows, you *were* perfect. Nobody even saw those tiny missteps. So what's the difference?"

Lisa sighed. "Maybe it didn't matter much this time," she said. "But sometimes, those tiny missteps can cost big. Like that B-plus I got, for instance. Right now everyone keeps saying it's no big deal, but they'll feel differently if it keeps me from being accepted at a top college."

"Don't worry, Lisa," Carole said. "When the time comes, I'm sure every college around will be knocking down your door to sign you up." She could tell that Lisa was still thinking a lot about her grade. That must be the real reason she was so upset about a few minor mistakes in her dance routine. Maybe now that she was moving into the same cabin with Carole and Stevie, they could

148

help her relax and enjoy herself a little more. After all, things were always better when The Saddle Club was together.

Stevie was thinking the same thing. She leaned back on her elbows and glanced at the driveway as another car came into view. This time it was a long, black sedan. "Hey, look," she said. "Isn't that the same car we saw by the road when we first got here?"

Carole looked. "The gangster's car?" she said. "It looks like it."

"I wonder which kid it's here for," Stevie said. She watched as the car pulled up and stopped next to the rec hall. The driver was hidden from view by some trees, and Stevie soon lost interest. She turned over onto her stomach and looked up at her friends. "You two are being very discreet," she teased. "You haven't even asked me about my walk with Phil."

"That's because we know you too well," Carole teased back. "We know you're going to tell us all about it sooner or later, whether we like it or not."

"Well, you're right," Stevie said, resting her chin on her hands and smiling dreamily. "And since you're so interested, I'll tell you right now. It was wonderful. He spent the first ten minutes apologizing. He said he didn't even realize how much time he was spending with Todd until it was too late." Her smile grew even dreamier. "He also said he would much rather spend time with me than with Todd—or anyone else, for that matter."

She didn't say anything more about it, but her dreamy smile told her friends everything they needed to know. Carole and Lisa traded amused glances. It was obvious that Stevie and Phil's romance was definitely back on and better than ever.

Just then, the girls heard the sound of another vehicle moving toward them. A moment later, a familiar horse van emerged from the trees.

"He's here!" Carole cried. "Starlight is here at last!" She jumped up and raced to meet the van.

Stevie and Lisa got up and followed. They could see Red's familiar face behind the wheel, and a moment later they all heard a familiar nicker from inside the van.

Carole could hardly wait as Red helped her lower the ramp and lead Starlight out. As she threw her arms around the big bay horse for a long-awaited hug, Carole thought she had never been happier. Starlight was here, Lisa was moving into Cabin Three where she belonged, and there were still two more weeks of camp to go, including the exciting show-jumping competition. She was ready to put the last two weeks of camp behind her and to make sure the rest of The Saddle Club's stay at Moose Hill Riding Camp was *totally* perfect.

About the Author

BONNIE BRYANT is the author of many books for young readers, including novelizations of movie hits such as *Teenage Mutant Ninja Turtles* and *Honey, I Blew Up the Kid*, written under her married name, B. B. Hiller.

Ms. Bryant began writing The Saddle Club in 1986. Although she had done some riding before that, she intensified her studies then and found herself learning right along with her characters Stevie, Carole, and Lisa. She claims that they are all much better riders than she is.

Ms. Bryant was born and raised in New York City. She still lives there, in Greenwich Village, with her two sons.

Don't miss Bonnie Bryant's exciting companion novel to
Summer Horse . . .

SUMMER RIDER
Saddle Club #68

Stevie Lake and Carole Hanson are thrilled that Lisa Atwood is finally being moved into their cabin. They're glad that Stevie and her boyfriend aren't arguing anymore. And they're relieved that Carole's horse, Starlight, has been shipped to the camp.

But Lisa still seems tense and unhappy about something. And her best friends have noticed that control-crazy Lisa seems to be working too hard on projects that are supposed to be fun. What could be wrong?

The last two weeks of camp should be carefree, but Stevie, Carole, and Lisa are afraid that Moose Hill might not reopen next summer. Who would want to close down their favorite riding camp? And can they find out before it's too late?